CANIS SAPIENS

Book I: The Ino Factor

Anthony Regolino

© 2016 by Anthony Regolino

All rights reserved. No part of this book may be reproduced, stored in a retrieval system or transmitted in any form or by any means without the prior written permission of the publishers, except by a reviewer who may quote brief passages in a review to be printed in a newspaper, magazine or journal.

The final approval for this literary material is granted by the author.

First printing

This is a work of fiction. Names, characters, businesses, places, events and incidents are either the products of the author's imagination or used in a fictitious manner. Any resemblance to actual persons, living or dead, or actual events is purely coincidental.

ISBN: 978-1-61296-647-2

PUBLISHED BY BLACK ROSE WRITING

www.blackrosewriting.com

Printed in the United States of America

Suggested retail price $16.95

Canis Sapiens is printed in Book Antiqua

This book is dedicated to the furry, four-legged beauties that have both fascinated and terrified mankind for centuries, causing our progenitors to seek a kinship with and form an identification with these majestic creatures, thus resulting in the legend of the werewolf. Special thanks go to Carrie V., for being an inspiration and offering words of support and encouragement. And finally, for DJ, this series' first and most devout fan.

CANIS SAPIENS

ONE

Dear diary: What do you wear on a date with a werewolf? Okay, so perhaps I was not going into this with the right frame of mind. But how serious could one be about an interview with a man who claims to be the wolf man? And not just the wolf man, but a spokesman for a clan of them living in secret right before the very eyes of the so-called "normal world," a clan representative of dozens, perhaps hundreds, supposedly spread out all over the world.

The interview was to take place in an office belonging to an associate friend of his, as he did not wish to leave any link to his and his people's possible whereabouts or habitat. The office was in an industrial center located on a nature preserve. I wonder if the woodsy locale was intentional, fulfilling certain preordained impressions about where a werewolf would live but perhaps being the exact opposite of where this modern-day clan chose to live, another smokescreen effort to keep their location hidden.

Oh listen to me, acting as if this were a legitimate possibility, that there really could be such a race, and that this man was other than what he probably was, a crackpot or eccentric oddball with nothing better to do than pull elaborate hoaxes or practical jokes on any gullible or unsuspecting fool that would take out time to listen. And here I was preparing for the evening as if I might be able to work this meeting into a story of some kind and perhaps make a name for myself in the journalist community. Ha! He said he chose me because I was unknown, because the "professionals" would call in help and try to "outscoop" him by digging up more dirt than he was willing to reveal, sabotaging his entire plans and laying waste to a community that would continue to be misunderstood unless he could prepare the way beforehand. Of course I realized that he actually chose me because any legitimate "professional" would have thrown him out of their office, not that I had one to throw him out of.

And then there was the possibility that I was surprised hasn't occurred to me before. Staring at myself in my full-length bathroom-door mirror, noticing the way I looked as the towel I had wrapped around myself shifted and dipped slightly as I readjusted the one I wound about my wet head, it occurred to me what other possible motive the man could have had for wanting to lure me to a deserted cabin in the woods in the dead of the night... But this all somehow seemed too elaborate for someone who merely wanted to attack me, and from what I knew such assaults were usually carried out impulsively, as acts of passion. I dried myself off thoroughly, inserted a fresh tampon, and walked about my apartment looking for just the right apparel, something than exuded professionalism without suggesting mannishness. However, in case I was wrong about that *other* motive, I would try not to wear something that could cause unnecessary arousal—although I was aware that rapists and perverts need no help in that department, and I could dress as a cartoon Disney character and elicit the same response. I did intend to wear a skirt, however, due to my preference for comfort during this time of the month.

Fully dressed and with very little make-up, I headed out into the crisp, early evening air, wishing that I had time for dinner first. But a bag of grapes, easy to pick while driving, would have to suffice. I reached out to open the driver-side door of my little old VW bug, when I noticed the moon. It was full. I didn't know how such a detail could have escaped me before and wondered what kind of idiot in her right mind would keep an appointment with a self-proclaimed werewolf on the night of a full moon. The kind named Beverly Journal, I guess. But why should I have even bothered? What good could have come of this? I may have been desperate for a story with my name on a by-line, but shouldn't I have held out for one that could actually be printed in a paper other than a trash rag? Did I really think I could make news out of a tale (and after all, that's all this could be) of the plight of a pack of lycanthropes?

Then I considered the last piece I had worked on, exposing the town dump for not keeping to city safety ordinances. And the one before that where I attempted to ascertain the true source of the meat served in Den's Diner on Apricot Ave. After those hard-hitting [said with tongue in cheek] journalistic endeavors, back when I was a contributing reporter for my very small community paper, a night interviewing someone out of a classic Universal horror film would have made for a refreshing change of pace. Of course, if my present employer knew how I would be spending the evening, he would probably reconsider his reasons for hiring me, and then I would not even be worthy of my current job as fact-checker and copy editor. So I was brought back again to the same question: Why was I going?

Truth be told, I didn't have a better way to pass a Friday evening. Pathetic, isn't it? Far from unattractive (at least I like to think so, and so did my last employer, who found my appearance to be more than he could stand without touching me, and was thus the reason for my leaving), the last date I had was typical of most dates I was on, and I was always left with the conviction that I only attracted men who were interested in nothing more than being with a good-looking woman. When I'd inform them of my profession and ambition, they would think it's "cute" and I'd instantly want to head for the door. In fact, one man had put it perfectly on one date (our last) when he said, "A bod is a terrible thing to waste, and a mind is a terrible thing to have." He was referring to women only, of course, and this catch phrase seemed to represent the mindset of every man that I went out with.

But I was too young to be this jaded; I really hadn't put on nearly enough mileage to come to this conclusion so readily. It was just that the last event of this sort happened only three nights before. To be honest, before college I didn't date much, *at* college I was more concerned with working toward a career, and in the few years since graduating I seemed to be spending all my time searching for the right position and place to work, not the right man. But I had dwelt enough on this. I didn't begin this journal to write the kind of diary a teenage girl would confess all her late-night desires to. It was a professional tool for my current assignment—self-appointed though it may have been—and I intended to keep it filled with facts and events, not secrets and schoolgirl musings.

My bug hesitated before starting, and when I rolled my eyes toward the heavens wishing I could afford a better means of transportation, my eyes once again found the moon—bright, full, and staring down at me, as if mocking me by reminding me what it signifies. Yes, I knew all the popular lore about werewolves; my brother used to watch scores of shows on them, as well as owning toys and books that adorned his shelves and declared him quite definitively to be their number one fan. That was before he discovered girls and became a wolf himself.

I personally never saw the appeal. I have read vampire stories on occasion, and the classic *Frankenstein* and *Dr. Jekyll and Mr. Hyde*, but the thought of a person turning into Lassie always struck me as more than a trifle ludicrous, and it boggled my mind that it could actually thrill or scare anyone. Maybe it reminded me too much of Disney's *Shaggy Dog* films. Anyhow, impressed by it or not, I was familiar with it and planned to show off all my secondhand knowledge at my upcoming meeting. Perhaps I could get him off guard and mention something *he* didn't even know. Wouldn't *that* be something? A veritable layperson exposing the supposed expert to be a fraud! I was starting to look forward to this bizarre rendezvous. I looked up at that near-perfect round disc, getting brighter as the sky grew darker, and thought aloud, "Bring it on!"

It took an hour to get there, and there wasn't even much leftover from the rush-hour traffic of people on their way back from jobs in the city. And I thought *I* lived far from the city! The industrial center had a maze of buildings, but my interviewee told me he would be in the first office at the front of the grounds. A jeep was parked right outside the entrance, and I parked on the other side of it. I walked around the back of the other vehicle, glanced at the license plate (to see that it *was* from this state), and approached the door to the front office. Ignoring the doorbell and knocker, I tried the door and found it unlocked. I let myself in.

There he was. Middle-aged. Neatly but not expensively dressed. Sitting behind a desk, watching me quietly. I had not taken him by surprise at all. Sure I knew he must have heard my car on the dirt road, but I thought he would at least have been taken aback by my sudden intrusion. Most people surely would have knocked. He gestured to a seat across from him and I sat in it and began taking out my pad and tape recorder, the recorder for capturing his words and the pad for any observances I found noteworthy.

"Mister... ?" I began, pronouncing each syllable almost separately and holding the second one in a way that obviously meant I expected him to fill in the blank. He didn't bite.

"Professor will suffice."

"And just what are you a professor of?" I inquired, hoping that it didn't come out sounding too snide.

"Sociology," he answered, his tone rising to announce that he was not finished, "and history."

"And where did you get—"

"Miss Journal."

"Beverly," I volunteered, but I was not sure why. Somehow I felt at ease with him, a stranger claiming to be a wild creature at heart. "I hate my last name. Can't wait till I get married so I can change it. I mean, a writer named Journal; how tacky is that?"

I don't know why I was suddenly offering all this info in such an unprofessional manner. I felt foolish, like I suddenly presented myself as some giddy student who couldn't stop herself from running off at the mouth. I looked away, sat up straight, and turned my attention to my recorder to distract from the awkward moment, checking that the tape was inside when I knew full well that it was. It was an obvious pretense, and I am sure he was aware of it, but he politely ignored it and continued.

"Miss—" he began unconsciously, and then corrected himself, "Beverly, I don't wish to talk about such unimportant matters as my education and credentials. There is a greater issue here that needs to be revealed, and I feel you are the person to do it, and do it right."

"A greater issue," I repeated, clicking the recorder on to tape our conversation. "And that is... ?"

"The preservation of an endangered species."

"Werewolves," I ventured.

"That is correct."

"And why are they endangered?"

"For many reasons. After all, we have lived in hiding for so many centuries and have faced all sorts of obstacles. We do not live among you as such, not so completely, and so we have very little in terms of rights or property claims."

"I don't understand."

"Well, we have no social security numbers; we don't exist according to your society. Years ago, we learned to fake it and obtained things such as land and cars by preying on the dead."

"Your victims." I thought this a natural observation, but he seemed disturbed by it.

"Oh dear. You are obviously jumping to the wrong conclusions about us."

I shook my head and was about to defend myself when he held up a hand, licked his lips, swallowed, and began what I expected to be a lengthy explanation.

"You think us murderers. See, this is exactly why the truth about us must come out. How can we expect to enter your world if we're looked upon as the slaughtering monsters of your motion pictures?"

I opened my mouth to respond but he gave a quick shake of his head and continued at a steady clip.

"We are just a race of beings, like yourselves except from another species. We have the ability to shape-shift, as has been reported at great length by your Native Americans centuries ago, and because of it we have some techniques that could best be described as regeneration. Healing, growing back severed limbs..."

I could tell he was on a roll, but he was giving me too much too fast, and I found I had a question for every other word he said. Native Americans, centuries ago, shape-shifting, healing. I had to interrupt and tell him as much.

"You're right," he said, pausing and breathing more slowly and deeply. Now he would be clearer and easier to understand.

Wishing to start from the beginning, my obvious first question was: "Where did your race come from? You said that the Native Americans knew of you centuries ago. But how did it all begin?"

"Do you know where you originally came from? Exactly? Unfortunately, neither do we. As far as we can tell, we have been around as long as you, but who knows? No one kept records in the beginning, and then when they did start recording historical events—and I'm speaking of both our species—many were destroyed by natural disasters or war. Your scientists believe that you evolved from an animal that's a cross between human and ape, and then at some point there was a divergence, with a possible missing link in between, resulting in the two distinctly different, yet obviously related, species that exist today. Well, for us it's the wolf that we descended from. Just like *Canis lupus*, the common gray wolf. And our scientific name for what we are is *Canis sapien*."

"Are you sure you descended from wolves? You sure look a lot like us. Isn't it possible that you are an offshoot of *Homo sapiens* instead, perhaps the missing link you referred to? Wouldn't you then be considered *Homo lupus*?" I thought I was being very clever here, but he obviously didn't think so.

"*Homo lupus?* What an absolutely dreadful name. 'Homo' is such a derogatory word, these days especially, and 'lupus' as in the disease? What species would dare call itself by that name?"

"I sense more than a little derision in your tone. Have you something against homosexuals? Aren't there any among your species?" His reply was quicker than I expected.

"None that I am aware of. We are a species that abides by the laws of nature. Our sexuality, as with the rest of our lifestyle, is in commune with her laws, and we do not actively reject it or seek to destroy it, as some other species I will refrain from naming."

Oh great, an eccentric naturist. And here I thought I was rooting out some deep-seated prejudice that may exist in this head case. I was beginning to think that this was no joke and that he firmly believed what he was saying, and I wondered if I should be scared. I knew that the nature-destroying species he was referring to was my own, so I said thank you in response to his discretion. "Still, what makes you so sure you are not descended from man after all?"

"When we are born, we are canine. You see, we do not shape-shift *into* wolves; we shape-shift into man."

Now he lost me. All that I thought I knew about werewolves was right out the window. Or so I thought. "Wait a minute. I thought you had to be bitten by a wolf man in order to become one. So if you were born one, who was originally bitten among your ancestors?"

"No one. You have to be born into a species; you can't just become one. And as I was trying to say before, we don't go around biting people and turning them into werewolves. We are a peaceful, nature-loving species. Ya know, we never had this misconception from the Native Americans. They understood us better, and I think envied us our shape-shifting ability."

The confusion I felt must have been evidenced on my face, for he suddenly addressed the thing that perplexed me most. "All right. We do have our occasional deviant and sociopath, just as you do, but on a much smaller scale. And if he were to attack a human being, the result would be similar to what you see in your movies."

"He becomes a lycanthrope?" I queried, sticking in a term that I hoped he would be impressed I knew, for I was feeling like a lost child and needed some sort of show of intelligence. But he didn't even allow me that much.

"Lycanthropy is another unpleasant word we do not wish to use. Because of it's original usage—for certain deranged schizophrenics—it implies that a person only *thinks* he is a werewolf, when in fact we are." Always his tone was conversational, even friendly, especially when answering a challenging question. And I again forgot any previous worries I may have had regarding how dangerous he might be, and I found myself liking him more. He continued, "But the human who was bitten by one of us doesn't actually become one of us; as I have said, you must be born one. He does, however, obtain certain limited shape-shifting abilities, although he has no concept of how to control them. When the urge is greatest—when the moon is full—and he feels the strange desire calling to him to come and run with the pack in the fields, he doesn't understand what is happening to him and he loses himself in the transition, dissociating himself utterly, leaving only an uncomprehending animal with a strong passion and no knowledge of what to do about it. He doesn't know that he is supposed to hunt deer and rodents; he doesn't know about packs and pack hierarchy. All he knows is that he has fangs and claws, a means to satisfy any hunger, and that he is surrounded by creatures who shriek and flee from him, as deer do, or who hunt and chase him. Either way, they must be dealt with, and he now has the natural tools at his disposal to dispatch any foe. *They* are the beings your movie monsters are based on. Not us."

"Is there any cure?"

"Perhaps one day, when we are accepted among you and have access to facilities and equipment, funding, and your greatest scientific minds, we may discover a means of reversing the effect."

"Those poor creatures." Yes, I said it with feeling, and for the moment I was so wrapped up in his tale that I forgot that it was all just a story.

"I also tend to think that they attack humans because, being human themselves, they have a natural fear of even the smallest animal. I've seen humans run from chipmunks and squirrels, and I don't mean to laugh, but lacking claws and fangs you really are one of the most defenseless mammals on the face of the planet! I mean, even a swooping canary can send you ducking for cover with your hands over your head." I didn't know whether to be offended by his mirth or to pity him, for if he is nothing but a mental case, then he must have some very harsh feelings about himself for him to have adopted this pretense of being a superior being.

"We call them Dingoes," his words intruded on my musing, "and consider them an epidemic that needs to be contained. We don't go around 'making them' for fun, or as an experiment. And when they get out of control, we take care of it—we're very responsible."

"What do you mean 'take care' of it?" I asked, but somehow already knew the answer. "You murder them?"

"We prefer the term 'euthanize.'"

"Dingoes. Aren't they those wild dogs in Africa or something?"

"Australia, yes. Dogs that act like wolves. We use it as a derogatory name amongst ourselves. And for these hapless creatures I've described."

Fictitious or not, I didn't want to think about such a condition anymore and changed the subject. "So since the moon is full, does that mean you are going to turn into a wolf?"

"I don't need the moon to be full to do that. Shape-shifters shape-shift at will. It is the infected human that, not knowing how to do it on his own, finds the urge to be beyond his capacity to quell whenever the moon is full. We still don't really know why that is. Maybe it has something to do with the moon's gravitational pull, something most people don't realize is strong enough to act on us. It causes tides in the ocean; why shouldn't it have an effect on us too? Makes people more prone to violence, doesn't it? All those statistics about higher crime rates, and the coining of the term *lunatic*. Yes, I'll bet old Luna is responsible somehow."

A slight discomfort down below reminded me of how the moon affected me personally. My cycle seemed to parallel the moon's, which I understand to be rather common among women. In fact, I recalled reading how it is conjectured that the first astronomers might have been women, studying the moon to try to understand what connection it might have to their womanly cycles, for it was apparent to them that there must be a relation between the two, both having cycles that last a month long.

I found it interesting that he referred to "lunatics," when he was perhaps one himself. I still wasn't certain, and again felt useless. My major may have been Journalism, but I minored in Psychology and thought myself quite adept at reading people. True, I didn't much enjoy the curriculum; the only class I found absolutely engrossing was Abnormal Psych. II: Criminal Behavior. And I considered myself to be a bit of an amateur shrink, so it was frustrating to acknowledge that when I wasn't taken in by this Professor's congenial nature, I was taken in instead by the rich depiction of his fabrication—even to the point of nearly believing it at times! I just hoped I proved a better reporter than psychiatrist. Time to find out.

"So go ahead," I casually invited.

"Go ahead?" he repeated, suspecting but not quite sure what I meant.

"Yes, shape-shift. If you can do it at will, and you wish to prove to me that what you are saying is more than a remarkably well-crafted story, that would be a good way to do it. No?"

"Uh... no. If I were to do that, you'd include it in your story, wouldn't you?"

That seemed to make sense to me. "How else could I defend my article?"

"But that's just the thing. If you go off telling people that you saw a man turn into a wolf, you would lose all credibility. And that's not what we want. Their eyes just need to be opened to the possibility for now. It *is* a process that's going to take time. Years."

"Well how 'bout for me then? So that I know I am reporting something that I personally believe to be true."

"Oh you don't have to believe."

I waited a few seconds and then said, "You're not going to change for me, are you?"

"Sorry."

I felt we had reached an impasse. I hesitatingly reached toward the cassette recorder, actually just to make it look as if I was considering shutting it off, which would imply I was through with him and his tale, when in fact I was only trying to draw him out further. I think he saw right through that, though, and continued to sit quietly, in his comfortable, casually congenial pose.

"All right, there is something I haven't been up front about," he finally said, in a sincere tone with his head tilted forward and his eyes dropping to his lap. This should be good. "The things I am telling you, I am doing without authorization, without the pack's consent. I'm acting on my own." Okay this wasn't what I was hoping for, but maybe it'll lead to something. "There are many among us with very narrow vision, who can't or who refuse to see the big picture, which is that we *will* die off if we do not find acceptance in this world—*your* world. And unfortunately it is these narrow-minded individuals who are our leaders, our alpha personalities."

"I thought *you* were their leader."

"Oh heavens no," he seemed embarrassed and almost blushed. "I'm just an old dog who's... seen a lot of changes in his life. And I'd like to think I can finally do something for my people before my time is up."

"What are you talking about? You can't be more than..." I had no clue as to his age, but I was honest in my appraisal that he didn't strike me as being so old, ". . . fifty-five?"

"Fifty-two. Which is ancient for us. You know how short a dog's life span is. Well, we live longer than they do, but nowhere near as long as humans. No, one of the things you have over us is that you can live to an age nearly twice what we can. My time is short. We don't live for very much longer once we hit our fifties."

Another interesting element. If he *is* a candidate for the looney bin, not only did he make himself superior to his peers, but he robbed himself of many years of life. I couldn't help but come to the conclusion that he meant to kill himself. Why else would he declare that he hadn't much time left on this world? "Well, if you say so, but... it's hard to accept; you look like you are in great shape." And he did.

"That comes from a life of hardy exercise, running across the land. Plus, I'm a shape-shifter. Do you think someone who can control how he looks would intentionally give himself an out-of-shape appearance?" He laughed as he said this, but his smile was a sad one, though I don't think he meant it to be. I was again given the impression that he intended this night, or perhaps another not long from now, to be his last on this planet, so I decided to tackle that topic rather than let him return to what he seemed to think of as his earth-shattering revelation.

"Do you have an afterlife?"

This question caught him by surprise, and I must confess to a secret pleasure at this. But then he answered without another moment's hesitation: "We believe that we will run in some Elysian field, as in mythology, in our true form, alongside our cousins, the natural wolves."

"Do you actually look like them? Or some cross between them and us? If I saw you as a wolf, would I be able to tell I wasn't looking at a real wolf?"

"A very astute question," he said. "Both of them, in fact." I could tell that I had finally impressed him, but it wasn't with my knowledge of the folklore. "You would *not* be able to distinguish me from a natural wolf. Those half-man/half-animal images from your popular media are reminiscent of the Dingoes, who subconsciously fight the transition so fiercely that they often get stuck lingering somewhere between the two forms."

"All right, you like those questions, how 'bout this one: What if you bite an actual wolf? Or a rabbit, a mouse, any other animal on the face of the earth? Do they then become were-creatures too?" I was cookin' now, letting myself get into the mythos and explore the situation as if it were real. And that, I knew, was what finally had impressed him. Well, if the only way into his head was through his story, that was the path I'd have to take. Foolishly I thought that perhaps I had made the wrong choice and should have more carefully considered the prospect of pursuing psychotherapy as a career.

"No, only humans seem to be affected in this way. Surprising, actually, when you think about it. I mean, why you?"

This was followed by an unplanned silence, where both of us (or at least I) struggled to come up with what to say next. I was aware of the recorder taping nothing but that awful empty room sound that always sounds so inexplicably audible, and loud, when played back. He seemed to be elsewhere in his thoughts, to have momentarily forgotten me, and I sat quietly and observed him furtively, not wishing to distract him out of whatever mind frame he had fallen into.

My body was suddenly quivering, and it took me a few seconds to realize what had caused it. There was a deep rumble coming from somewhere inside the room, and as it grew in volume I realized that it was an animal growl—and it was coming from the Professor! I lost all sense of reality, or reality as I knew it before I walked into this fairy tale, and sat in stark terror waiting for him to do what I had previously wanted him to do, what I had asked him to do, what he told me he would *not* do for me—to change into an animal.

A furry head popped up from behind his side of the desk, and I relaxed and let go a breath I didn't know I was holding when I realized that the sound had come from an average dog, a German

Shepherd to be precise, that must have been lying at his feet the whole time. It stopped growling but was alert and staring at the side window, which the Professor was keenly watching as well. I found the whole scene to be eerily disturbing, especially when I realized that whatever was out there was picked up by the man's senses before the animal's. He had stopped speaking moments before the dog's warning came, back when I mistakenly thought he was as stumped for what to say next as I was.

"It's all right, Ginger, just an uninvited rodent," he said soothingly, stroking the dog's head affectionately. I confess I found this odd, but couldn't quite explain the reasons for feeling that way. This was abundantly clear in my stammering.

"You have a—You have a dog?" He nodded. "But you're—I mean, what could she be to..." How to put it delicately? Fortunately he saved me from any further embarrassing remarks.

"Not a mate, if that's what you're thinking, although in wolf form some members have been known to run with true wolves and... spend the night with them. Just as in human form some have taken human women to bed. It's more a form of... How do they say it these days? Sexually experimenting? But no, *Canis familiaris*, the domestic dog, is almost like what cats are to witches: our familiars. You see, we are related to them, so they are more than pets to us. Sort of like how you humans view chimpanzees, your closest relatives in the Animal Kingdom."

He seemed to have glossed over something that I found to be infinitely more intriguing, and might perhaps reveal a flaw in his earlier reasoning. "You said you have to be born one to be one of you. What about when one of you mates with my kind? Wouldn't the offspring be 'born one'? Perhaps you aren't descended from the wolf after all. What if—"

"We cannot impregnate you. We are, after all, from two vastly separated species."

I couldn't accept that. "You mean there's *never* been a case—"

"Not to be vulgar, but I have as much a chance of getting you pregnant as your kind has of impregnating Ginger here." He patted the dog's head and observed her with renewed interest, I think because he was slightly embarrassed by the direction our conversation had suddenly taken. He continued watching and petting his companion as he spoke. "As I said before, we are born in our true forms, and we give birth in that form. They are natural deliveries, so we are forced to get by under primitive medical conditions that your race has left far behind, replaced by better care and equipment. We have our own 'doctors,' of sorts. They hold no degree and their education is from confiscated books and mostly trial-and-error.

"Before, when I mentioned 'preying on the dead' and you thought I meant that we go around killing people and taking their things, what I was trying to say was that we, just like true wolves, *scavenge* from the dead. From necessity, we visit the homes of people who have passed away to obtain things that we need. Money, computers, other provisions, and occasionally, when we can get away with it, land. We have no social security numbers. In this modern age, we cannot even get a job without that! But recently, with computers, and the Internet especially, we have been able to anonymously enter into business transactions, locate land that we can stake a fraudulent claim on, try to accumulate enough of this 'money' that your race has wrongfully instituted upon this unfortunate world. Money! Nothing good has ever come of it; it is a scourge on this planet that has ruined and killed more people than religion or anything else that runs people's lives."

I didn't know if that were true or not; I certainly know many historians and war buffs who would eagerly dispute him on that, but he did seem to make sense. Given that the absurdly high numbers of deaths attributed to religion usually came about in spurts during wars, jihads, and other forms of mass cleansings, if there were a way to total up the ongoing death tolls that occur every few minutes from muggings, holdups, and all other elaborate methods man has concocted to rob his brother of his hard-earned wages, the figures would probably put to shame any claims of devastation that all the wars put together could boast of. But then, this was sheer conjecture on my part, and I suspect on his part as well. I didn't have time to consider this further at the time, for he continued immediately with his lament.

"If I sound bitter, it is because of the struggles that we have had to endure just to survive and try to inhabit the bounteous land that nature has provided, and that man is continually taking away. Don't we have just as much right to it? At least with the Native Americans you are trying to make amends and at least have reservations for them. Don't we deserve the same?"

I didn't know what to say. Not believing any of his story, I found all this to be unimportant and moot, albeit interesting in a fictional way — he did plot out all the things that such a race would have to face. And unfortunately he had a lot more to say about this, occasionally sprinkled with the interesting oddity that interested me more.

"We use whatever tactic we can get away with, phony inheritance claims working best until the land is discovered by some developer who takes a fancy to it. Well, we can't back it up or take it to court. Our claim proves shaky under even the thinnest of investigations, and we must abandon our homes en masse to some new ground, leaving some lucky developer to exploit the land and its resources for not even a song."

"But what about all the money you said you collect?"

"We have no interest in material wealth or worldly possessions. The call of the wild lures us more than the smell of cash. What we see as a fortune is nothing more than a drop in the bucket to your people. And besides, we can't purchase and establish a real community within one of your towns because of the exposure. We need the isolation. Unless, as I hope, we can introduce ourselves to the world openly and be accepted for what we are. And I believe the time may be right for that now. It wouldn't be 'politically correct' to discriminate against us, or to deny us the opportunity to enjoy life, liberty, and the pursuit of happiness in our own homeland. And after all, like the Native Americans, we *were* here before you."

"Why did I think you came from England?" I muttered, probably recalling films of fog-covered moors and the inevitable werewolf attacks.

"You're thinking of Warren Zevon," he said, and then after noticing my confused expression added "*Werewolves of London.*"

"Oh. You must hate all our films. And that song too."

"Not at all," he replied. "Some are very entertaining. And I especially like that song. '*Li*ttle o*l*' *l*ady got muti*l*ated *l*ate *l*ast night.' Great use of alliteration."

I couldn't tell if he was serious or putting me on. "Right," I said, in a way meant to convey my uncertainty.

"And you should hear some of *our* stories. We have our own version of *Little Red Riding Hood*—but perhaps you wouldn't appreciate that one."

Now I was sure he was kidding me.

"Well, I think you have all you need for your first installment," he said, and I wasn't sure I heard him correctly. Was he dismissing me? "We'll... and by 'we'll' you already know I mean 'I'll' contact you after gauging the reactions this first piece generates."

"Wait a minute. You think I can actually get in print with what little you've given me? You may know about your little werewolf community and all, but you don't know very much about journalism. At best, I could maybe sell a story to some sci-fi magazine or pitch a movie with what you've offerred so far, but this is not ready for the news. I need to see this place, take pictures, interview—"

"Now you know I can't authorize that. As I've confessed, I am doing this without their knowledge. There's no way I could sneak you in, even at a distance; they'd smell you a mile away. And that's assuming I would consider exposing our location, which I've already told you is out of the question. It's forbidden."

"So was talking to me."

There it was again, that low, deep grumble that still sent shivers and left me feeling hollow inside despite my knowing its source. The dog was growling again, not looking at the window but somewhere off in space, and I can only conclude that she was responding to our voices, which had risen in our excitement.

I snatched up my things, the renewed scare from the dog suddenly making me want to get out of this place as quickly as possible. He spoke to my back as I headed rudely for the door I came in through. "Sorry," he said. "But you're gonna have to trust me on this. It *will* be enough for now."

I was out the door and, after closing it behind me, I remained on the outside porch breathing in deeply the fresh, woodsy night air. I may not have been inside for long, but the sky had grown dark very quickly. I clicked off the still-running recorder, struggled to open my bag so I could put the machine and my notepad inside, and instead managed to drop the recorder onto the wood flooring. I bent down and examined it, hoping that it didn't get damaged or that the tape didn't somehow break, and when I stood up I was facing a man.

I should have heard his approach but didn't. I tried to rationalize it by suggesting to myself that I was too wrapped up with retrieving and checking the fallen instrument, but deep inside another, undefined suspicion was playing at the back of my mind, one which I steadfastly refused to acknowledge. He looked hard into my eyes, with a smile that was sinister and utterly devoid of warmth. His hair was long, black waves covering and slightly passing the bare, well-muscled shoulders that were exposed by his sleeveless shirt, which I thought was too brief for this chilling autumn night. I must confess, however, that I would have found the look very appealing if it were not for the harsh features of his face. "Excuse me," I mumbled, not knowing what else to say. I became aware of more men emerging from the darkness. The one in front of me glanced back at them and gave a slight toss of his head toward the cabin. They suddenly disappeared behind the sides of the cabin, and I had the definite impression that he had dispatched them to surround the place. I made a step to the side so that I could pass him, but it was countered by a move of his own. He obviously was not going to let me pass.

"So what's that old dog been telling you?" he asked, again looking directly into my eyes with an intensity that made it hard for me to meet his gaze. "He been telling stories about his family again? You know he's quite certifiable. But the family is an old-fashioned one that likes to take care of their own. You understand? So what did he say about them?"

"A reporter and her source enjoy the same type of confidentiality as in a doctor/patient relationship." I don't know where I summoned the courage from to answer him in that way; I certainly didn't feel brave in his presence.

The smile abruptly vanished from his face, and his tone changed as he asked his next question. "Did he say we were really wolves?"

I took a step back and stepped on someone's toes. The tape recorder dropped from my hand as I looked back quickly and saw a woman wearing a smile that matched the one he had previously worn. Her flawless face was framed by luxurious brunette hair that was so rich it almost looked black, especially in this late hour. Its dark ringlets contrasted with my straight blonde hair, offering a stark contrast between us. "I'm sorry," I said weakly. She said nothing and kept her smile in place, and I decided that I liked her even less than the man.

"Ah-ooo!"

I turned back even quicker to find him laughing and imitating a wolf howling at the moon. "Ah-ooo!" came the woman's answering cry from behind me, but I refused to look back at her and give her the satisfaction of having frightened me as well.

"What else does a wolf do?" he playfully asked. He bent down to pick up the twice-fallen object, and then dropped down into a crouch—not to his hands and knees but just balancing on the balls of his feet, which like the woman's were covered in sandals. He started sniffing, and then plunged his nose into my crotch, sniffing in fiercely again and again.

I was mortified. Aside from the mental torment and the physical—or rather sexual—harassment he was inflicting, I was also conscious of my period and embarrassed by the smell I must have been giving off down there. I imagined that the blood was flowing very heavily at that moment. I again backed up into the woman, and when my arms automatically flew out for balance, she locked hers around mine and held them back. I wondered about the Professor and his dog. Surely he must be hearing all that was going on outside his door. Why wasn't he here, at least to threaten them with the German Shepherd?

A sudden blast of air, as a dog does when it snorts out, warmed my crotch mercilessly, and after he sniffed a few more times and snorted out again, I must confess that my body was inappropriately basking in the sensuous nature of the sensation. It had been a while since anyone was down there, and the feeling generated by the caress of his stubble-laden jaw and the hot gusts emitted from his nostrils, even through the material of my skirt and panties, was enough to trick my vagina into responding. I cursed it silently and fought the sensation, then became aware of a crashing noise and of loud sounds emanating from far back inside the cabin. I felt it must have been the Professor encountering those men, and knew that he would not be coming to my aid.

The man rose in front of me and I winced at the faint smell—my smell!—that had tainted his face. He held out the recorder to me and stepped back. I didn't know if he were letting me go—he couldn't possibly be—but I felt the woman release her firm grip around my arms and so I took advantage of the opportunity. I accepted the instrument, daintily placed it inside my bag without yet moving, then ventured a step or two toward the porch steps and, when he didn't move to pursue, descended them and hurried to my parked vehicle. I fumbled with extracting the keys from my bag, realizing that I should have removed them when I had it open before. I watched as they stepped down as well and very slowly, very casually began walking in my direction. I felt lightheaded and dizzy; my breaths were rapid and shallow. I was hyperventilating and could no longer focus on them to see if they were approaching or not. I passed out.

TWO

I smiled at the refreshing scent of the woodsy outdoors. I wondered how I could smell that so clearly from my bed; must've left the bedroom window opened. But still, it never smelled like that before. When I suddenly recalled the events of the evening and of my last waking memory, I snapped open my eyes and looked around.

I was in my car, in the shoulder lane of the main road pointing home. I toyed for a moment with the notion that everything had been a dream, but knew better than that. A sudden breeze stirred up a slip of paper that began flapping in the breeze from where it was trapped under the driver's-side windshield wiper. A ticket? How long could I have been here? No, if it were a ticket, the police officer would've woken me up, not just left it there for me to find. Then there would have been questions...

I reached out through the open side window, lifted the paper from beneath the blade, and withdrew it inside to inspect. There were words on the page, printed in simple block letters, leaving no definable handwriting to trace. It read: FORGET ALL THIS EVER HAPPENED. THIS IS FOR YOUR OWN GOOD. YOU HAVE BEEN WARNED.

Perhaps if it didn't end with such a veiled threat I might have been able to let it go, but I tend to get rather confrontational when treated so boldly, whether for my own good or not. I made up my mind. I turned the car around and went back down the path that led to the front office of the industrial park to find out what had happened in the time that I was unconscious. I hoped the Professor was all right.

When I approached the building again, the same vehicle was parked in front, so I assumed he must still be there. This time I checked the registration sticker and found that it had expired about three months ago. I began to think how that fit in with his story, how this car would have been taken from someone who had died and how they would not have been able to renew the registration—then I realized how ridiculous I was being. Just because men came after him didn't make his story true, a story which couldn't possibly be true!

I listened at the door, then stopped myself from calling out to him in case the others were still lurking about. I remembered how I had barged in earlier and decided to do so again. I pushed the door open as quietly as I could and looked inside. I tasted bile.

The blood was all over, the Professor nowhere to be seen. But as I gazed all about at the red-drenched interior I felt a pang of pity as my eyes fell upon the Professor's companion, Ginger, or what was left of her. The German Shepherd was as still as any corpse could be. "How could they do that to a dog?" I wondered, and then noticed the body of another dog behind the desk, one that I couldn't see well enough and had to venture further inside in order to see better, forcing me to tread on the newly spilt blood, which now effectively ruined my favorite pair of shoes.

But this dog looked nothing like Ginger; it was a different breed, a husky maybe, or a malamute. Except that the face... I was no expert on canine species, but I suddenly knew I was looking at no dog. This... was the dead body of a wolf. And I couldn't help but feel that I had found the Professor, his body reverted back to its natural form. I couldn't take my eyes from him; he really was a beautiful animal.

"Couldn't stay away, could ya?" came a voice from behind me. *His* voice. The one who had tormented me before. I turned and looked at him, and didn't bother trying to hide the rage I felt toward him and his kind, to have done this to one of their own. I don't know why this was enough, but seeing the mutilated canine bodies had convinced me that everything I had been told was true. That these were *Canis sapiens*.

"Coulda bet money on you comin' back here," he said nonchalantly, glancing over his shoulder at one of the men who flocked around him yet managed to hang back, leaving him always in the forefront. If I had to guess, I would've pegged him as their "alpha" leader. "Well, anyway, perhaps it's a good thing that you came back. I really should have had more of a chat with you about all this." The sound of a chair being dragged from the desk came from behind me, and I *knew* that it was the female once again lurking behind my back. The chair was positioned directly behind me, and her fingers pressed gently but firmly down on my shoulders until I was seated. "Now, about that raving old dog—"

"What did you do to him?" I asked, my voice coming out in a harsh rasp.

"Relax. You won't have to worry about him any longer." His smug tone confirmed what I already knew.

"So you *euthanized* him?" I exploded. "Or is that an expression you only use for Dingoes?" That stopped him in his tracks. He stood with his mouth open, clearly stunned, and shifted his gaze to exchange a worried look with the person behind my chair.

Finally he blew out a breath he had evidently been holding. "Well, looks like we were right to kill him. He obviously said too much."

It was the blatant admission of his crime, plus the rope that suddenly swung about my chest and arms, pinning me to the chair, that brought forth the height of my fury: "KILL! Kill? Using the big words now, are we? Kill, not 'euthanize'? You're no better than we are. You plot and conspire behind each other's backs, and then kill each..."

I broke off as he moved in front of me and bent down to sniff me again. He concentrated on my throat and chest area, but my loins once again betrayed my will by moistening in anticipation. Sometimes I hated being a woman.

He snapped to his full height and appraised me with what looked like admiration. "You are strong," he said. Well I felt anything but strong at the moment, but I knew he didn't mean physically. "You've masked the fear from your face and your voice," he elaborated, "but I can smell it on you as strongly as if you were crying hysterically. You want to be as good as us, you'll have to learn how to hide that too. And as for being 'as bad as you,' tell me, would one of you do this to one of us?"

He extended his left hand, and his index finder suddenly seemed unnaturally long. Then I realized that it wasn't the finger but the nail, which was growing into a sharpened claw, a deadly weapon. I had wanted proof of their shape-shifting ability and here it was, right before my very eyes, and I wondered if that would be the last thing I see as he stabs that blade into some tender part of me to pierce some vital organ. He placed the tip of his nail between my breasts, just above my heart and the rope that held me helpless. With a flick of his finger the rope snapped and fell apart, leaving me unfettered... and confused.

"Now I don't want to see you again," he stated simply, with mock politeness. "Please don't be offended; it's not the company, it's the situation. Aryana will escort you to your car, drive you back to the main road as before." His tone changed along with his expression, which grew sinister as he added, "This time, take it."

The brief ride was uncomfortable for me, doubly so because of my chauffeur, whom I felt a hatred for to a degree I had never experienced or known possible. I don't know why I felt as strongly as I did about her. It was partly because of her insolent smile and the way she handled me as if I were insignificant. But I was afraid to admit that it was in part because I might have been slightly envious of her position at his side. She was his right hand and a very competent one at that. She represented all that a woman could become in a man's world, but on the most basic, gut level, and yet I despised her for it. She made the trip slightly easier for me by not saying a word and concentrating only on the path ahead, and when we reached the road there was a pickup truck waiting there with some of the more wilder-looking members of her pack out in the back leaning over the side and leering at me amusedly. She put the car in park and turned to me with that awful smile that seemed to be her only means of communication. For all I knew she may not even have a voice, but between her lips and those eyes she was able to say exactly what she felt without any words being needed.

She slinked out of the car with a grace that was so sexually charged it gave me but another reason to be jealous, and she sauntered over to the wild men with strides akin to a dancer's strut. She climbed into the back among them with a confidence I knew *I* would not have had among that horde, and casually leaned over to join them in staring at me, all the while wordlessly exuding a power over them that again made me admire—and despise—her for her position in their world. The man who coined the term "weaker sex" would blanche in her presence and be forced to reconsider that opinion, as well as the expression that has outlived him and made women the world over chafe to hear that inferior generalization.

I don't know how long after they left in their pickup, back the way she had taken me, that I remained in my car sitting in the passenger seat, but I couldn't decide what to do next. I could not leave, but driving back would be as conspicuous as a rhino trying to sneak into a kiddie pool unobserved. I had to make it *look* like I was leaving and then hide the car and come back on foot, hiding amidst the trees while they concluded their business there. Not only did I want to see what they had planned next, but I wanted to get back inside that office and see the mess and the carcasses again. I needed to make sure they were what I thought they were, and not some hoax put on by these very convincing eccentrics. Sure the trick with his fingernail was impressive, but it could just as easily have been some elaborate prosthetic or a magician's or make-up effects maker's prop. I wasn't going to let them treat me like some gullible bimbo, when I was clearly not. This was far from over.

I found the perfect place to ditch my bug and made my way back with some difficulty, for the uneven road was not kind to the heels of my once-good shoes, and there was no question of attempting to cross the terrain without them. I arrived at the spot where the main road meets the path leading into the grounds, the place where I had been abandoned twice already, and peered into the forest of trees that fronted the natural preserve to see if I could approach the industrial center within without being seen, and without getting lost.

Confident that I could, I moved into the woodland region and slowly made my way in the direction I believed the front office to be. I progressed extremely slowly, as I could not maneuver well in my chosen footwear, and because I was hoping to catch them on their way out so I could have the place to myself for some time. Since I had no idea how much longer they intended to stick around, but feeling that people who had just committed murder would not stick around for very long, I allowed myself to procrastinate a bit.

A snap of a twig distracted me and sent a shiver up my spine as I glanced nervously around for what might have been its cause. I looked for an owl or a snake, and prayed that it wasn't one of those wild-looking men. It would be just my luck to have one stumble upon me as he slipped off to relieve himself in the outdoors. But I couldn't find the source of the disturbance, and so waited before proceeding a few more paces. I was counting my progression according to number of trees past, and so it was five trees before I heard another, similar sound. An unsettling feeling enveloped me, and I attempted to amuse myself to lighten my mood by inventing a twist to an old riddle: *If a woman falls in the woods and no one's there to hear her, does she make a sound?* It made me feel worse.

Another, louder sound followed, one that startled me so badly that I cried out with a terror that paralyzed me and left me clinging to the trunk of the tree in front of me. It was a human voice; it was *his* voice. "You're not going to be satisfied until you completely understand our plight, are you?"

The voice came from over my shoulder, and as I peered behind me with my head shaking so badly it hurt my neck, I saw him standing practically on top of me. How he was able to approach so near without my knowing bothered me immensely, leaving me feeling like I failed something very important in life, more important even than falling in love or earning money. Funny how they don't nurture survival instincts or teach self-preservation techniques in school.

"I can see that there is only one way we are going to convince you we are serious," he added, allowing me to turn around and look him in his eyes, eyes that reflected a green light in an animal way. The rest of his face was in shadow, and it was only his outline that I could make out, but his outline was unmistakable. Or at least it was a moment ago. Now it suddenly shifted and distorted, the edges growing hazy and fluid at the same time. He turned his face up to the sky and I could see the muzzle of a wolf extending from his face. I wondered if I were dreaming, and at what point the dream began. Just what part of this evening really did happen, or was I still at home, having fallen asleep before ever leaving for my meeting with the Professor?

The muzzle lowered and turned toward me. His silhouette grew as he lunged forward. I automatically snapped backward, but slammed into the nearby tree hard, feeling the pain of the trunk against the back of my head at the same time that I felt a pair of sharp teeth close onto my left shoulder. I didn't know which hurt more, but suddenly none of that mattered anymore, and as I slid down the tree feeling sparks of pain like fire all over my upper body, I prayed that my death would be mercifully quick.

THREE

I woke to the sound of a wolf howling. In a camping tent I lay, on bare earth and with a knapsack for a pillow. A female voice from outside said, "She's awake," and the tent's flap was immediately pushed aside so that my assailant could come in. I thought of him as my murderer, but technically I wasn't dead... yet. He was smiling and very pleasant to me, with not a trace of the smug sadistic charm he was trying to work on me earlier that evening. But of course my hatred would not be abated. I did my best to struggle to a sitting position, though my mind and body were still fatigued and fighting it.

"Glad to see you're awake. We've got plenty of ground rules to cover, and then I'll show you to your room," he said, then added, dramatically I thought: "And thus begins your life as a werewolf."

"Don't you mean a 'Dingo'?" I said, and to my own surprise I heard myself pronounce the word with the same distasteful prejudice that the "true" werewolves were supposed to have for them.

"Yes, you're so right. A Dingo. I don't know what impression you've got from our misguided old professor friend, but they *can* get by with our support, and they *do* serve a function in our community. We take great responsibility for the Dingoes we create, and you can rest assured that you will be looked after."

"Oh I feel so much better," I said sarcastically.

"You should. As you probably were told, Dingoes are considered a detrimental factor to our lifestyle. They don't pose a physical threat to us, but they run the risk of exposing us, should they get out of hand. So we work closely with them to make them feel like a contributing member of the pack."

"Yes, I know how important that is among wolves. Any injured or elderly member is expected to go off somewhere and die, aren't they?"

"Certain *human* tribes practiced such a custom, but no, we do not do such things. Regardless of what actual wolves may or may not do, we are more cultured, intelligent, and refined. If you want to draw comparisons, then should I expect you to throw your feces around at each other at the dinner table the way your less-advanced cousins in the animal kingdom do?"

Okay, he had me there. But I still had one very important question to ask and wanted to keep up my hostility for its delivery. "By the way," I began, almost casually, "why the hell *did* you bite me? I'm assuming it was you, wasn't it?"

"Yes. Me. Guilty as charged. But you can blame yourself for that. How many times did I let you go? You wouldn't walk away. So... I decided that the only way you would take our cause seriously... is if you had a vested interest in it. Something at stake."

"I pick my own causes," I replied.

"Well now you don't," he said, with a tone of impatience that reminded me of his former demeanor. I wasn't sure I really wanted his currently assumed congenial behavior—if assumed were all it was—to drop, for I knew how fierce he could appear and didn't think I could hold my own against him when he was like that. The only thing I had going for me was this "responsible" attitude he said they have toward their victims, and if that was why he was trying to be nice to me I had better let him act accordingly.

"I'm sorry," I said, rather blandly and without looking at him, and hoping that it would be enough for him that I make the effort without actually meaning it.

"All right, forget it," he said, and I silently blew a sigh of relief. "The important thing for you to know is that there *is no turning back*. There is no cure, no magic potion; your life among the humans has ended."

"And now I must live with my murderer?" He was about to attack my choice of wording, but I wouldn't let him begin. "I know, I'm *not dead*. But you just said it, my human life has ended. And you ended it."

He swallowed that, nodded, and proceeded as if I didn't interrupt him. "You'll be living as part of my pack. In this community at present there are five packs coexisting on the grounds we are currently occupying, but when we are forced to move, the only ties that remain unbroken are those to your pack. If we join up with any of the other packs again, it is simply for the sake of convenience and survival of the species. The community consists of 56 adults, numerous pups, and 15 other Dingoes beside yourself. You will see that they have completely adapted to our lifestyle and, in some ways, even prefer it to their old ones. *You* might, as well."

I wanted to mutter "Don't hold your breath" but held that comment because I didn't know how much longer his patience would hold out, and I might have wanted to jab him with another zinger at some point. He seemed to wait a moment for the retort he obviously expected from me, and when none came forth he was pleased and continued. I must admit that I did find all this information captivating, and wanted to remember all the details in case I had my chance to escape and tell the world of this experience.

"We don't," he began, and seemed to have difficulty proceeding, "have anything against you. It is not our intention to overrun the planet and replace your kind. We don't seek to make a whole bunch of raving Dingoes to set free upon the land. We're nothing like you've pictured us in your popular media."

"I know. The Professor explained this to me convincingly. *Your* actions, not just to me but to him, have colored a different impression on me though." He took that in, so I gave him another spoonful: "And if you want me to believe that you don't *kill* your victims..."

"We don't," he interjected. "On the occasion that one of us, for some reason or other, attacks one of your kind, the attacks are usually not fatal."

"Ah but they are!" I said loudly. "Because if there is no way to reverse it, and if Dingoes fit so easily in your community, then why would they need to be 'euthanized'? The Professor told me how those half-human, half-animal forms that we based our movie monsters on are actually Dingoes, how they hunt and run wild because they don't know how to control the changes and then can't deal with the transformation afterward, mentally or emotionally. Face it, you killed me tonight. It's just gonna take a while for me to die." That was the zinger I wanted to deliver, and I relished every second of it. Then something occurred to me. "Hey, it's still dark out. Why aren't I changing into some monster?"

"It's a little after 2:00 a.m., but since you were only just bitten on this night your body still has to undergo the changes that will allow it to transform into a wol—into something *between* a wolf and a human."

"Right, because we can't actually change into a wolf, just some brainless creature."

He looked down, almost sadly I thought, and nodded his agreement. "We have scientists working to try to curb the desires, to try to reason with the Dingo while in the beast stage, but we're still a long way off from domesticating them while they're like that."

"And *you* can turn into a wolf completely. No in-between monster stage?"

"That's right. We are shape-shifters. That is in our nature."

"Then why were you on two legs when you bit me? Why weren't you down on all fours?"

"Convenience. I wanted to reach you easier without having to leap and risk damaging you worse than I intended. So I just changed part of my body. We *can* do that, you know. Well, *we* can do it; *you* cannot."

"Why worry about damaging me? Don't I have 'rejuvenating

abilities' or something now?"

"I'm sure the Professor told you how limited they are. And they take time. Lots of time, if the wound is severe enough. And it hurts the whole way through. I know. When I was little more than a pup, sort of an adolescent upstart just waiting to challenge for the alpha spot, I got snared in a trap that some hunters laid out in the woods. They were coming. My pack wasn't around to help. Well, you've heard how a wolf will bite his leg off to escape a trap. Well I damn near did that. What was left of the leg was a shambles. But I escaped the hunters. When I made it to my pack, they had to cut it off entirely so it would grow back right. I stayed in that condition for three weeks before I had something strong enough to walk on, and then it took another week for the pain to end and for it to be totally healed. Believe me, you don't want to risk any damage to your body on the basis that 'it'll grow back' or 'it'll heal itself.'"

I sat fascinated by his story, and actually felt for my assailant just then. He looked at me, and then offered me another courtesy. "Look, you're probably tired. This can all wait till the morning if you want. I only came in here because you woke up. You just can't interact with anyone until I've made everything clear for you."

I noticed that the outside howling had stopped, but didn't know how long ago that happened. I wasn't at all tired, and the pain in my shoulder, which I finally realized was bandaged up, was minimal. I *needed* to know more, and begged him to go on.

"Okay," he grudgingly consented. "At some point you're going to be assigned a name—"

"Excuse me?"

"When we are in wolf form, we can't speak English. Our true names are in a tongue you cannot speak, but you could understand certain sounds, and your name in our language is one that you are required to learn. Trust me, it's a necessity in emergency situations. And it wouldn't be difficult for you to make out; it'll be a combination of very distinct sounds, something even a human could distinguish."

The thought of being assigned a name offended me deeply. I know I said that I didn't like my name anyway, but I didn't think "yip-woof-bow-wow-arf" would be an improvement.

"And as for what to call us, we all have adopted human names, just as we all have a human form. You can call *me* Jack."

A sudden, discomforting thought hit me. "Let me get this straight. About this shape-shifting, can you walk out of here and simply come back in another shape, or with another face, or skin color, or sex?" The thought of never knowing who anyone really was and than Jack and Aryana could be next to me without my knowing was extremely unsettling.

"No. We cannot switch gender, or physical appearance, or even body color. For us to develop a human form requires a commitment to that form, for our body to mold it into our psyche so that adopting it becomes second nature. How physically fit we are in our true form determines how fit we are in human form."

So much for my notion that they look so beautiful because they can just *make* themselves look as fit or as attractive as they want. My resentment for the perfect Aryana grew further.

"You probably already know about how the full moon brings out the urge in Dingoes so much that they can't control it. But you have nothing to fear. You will be sedated and locked up for extra measure to prevent your doing harm to yourself or anyone else. You'll simply sleep through it and wake up the next morning, having no memory of any troubled sleep should you indeed experience anything." The howling outside returned, one single voice seemingly in torment. It grew in urgency to a terrifying peak, then ceased as abruptly as it began.

"Yes," he confirmed, "what you're hearing is a Dingo whose will is fighting the drug we use. He might need a stronger dosage next time, or an alternate medicinal choice. There are more efficient formulas, but acquiring them isn't always easy, and when possible we prefer using natural ingredients that we can grow ourselves. Some of these may be of the... hallucinogenic kind, but you wouldn't be aware of any of their effects because at the time you wouldn't be yourself anyway." He smiled, then grew serious and added, "Only rarely does one get so out of control that he needs to be put down. Euthanized, as you like to keep mentioning."

"How? Wouldn't anything you do to it just heal over time?"

"Here's where myth and reality agree. For some reason we cannot expunge argentum from our system, and it is fatal to us. As long as it gets into our bloodstream, there is no cure we know of. And believe me, our best minds are working on it, but our best scientific minds are years behind your own, and it's just something we've come to accept down through time as being our one weakness. Our Kryptonite. Everyone has to have an Achilles' heel, right? Even vampires."

"You're not going to tell me vampires are real too, are you?"

"No. Not as far as I know. But then maybe they exist somewhere and don't know that *we* exist. It's a possibility. So they have their crosses and garlic, their stakes and beheadings and fire, and we have argentum."

"Argentum?" I repeated, recognizing the word from chemistry class but not exactly recalling what it was. I hoped I didn't appear too unintelligent to him.

"Yes, argentum. Silver." Of course. "So now you know our weakness. But remember... it's now *your* weakness too. Your body chemistry is changing to adapt elements of ours."

"So silver *does* kill a werewolf. What about jewelry? What happens if you come into contact with it?" I asked, suddenly uncomfortable about the silver earrings I had in my earlobes. After all, they weren't just touching my skin but piercing through my flesh.

"That's fine; you can touch it all you want. We're only talking about when it gets into our bloodstream. So your earrings won't kill you where they are, in those fleshy lobes with their holes healed over long ago," he answered, reading my mind. "But if you were to use the point to prick a major artery," and here he hesitated, knowing that I was desperately hanging on his every word, "yes it could kill you. You might want to think about wearing natural jewelry, as most of us do. If you were to walk around town with that, it would be the equivalent of a person entering a subway car with a knife, or a kid taking a gun to school. It's frowned upon."

I instantly took them out and placed them in my bag, which was on the ground next to me with my tape recorder, making sure that the points were securely capped first. It was exhilarating to know that I had with me a weapon, the power to kill them, to take the lives of my captors should the need, and opportunity, arise.

"There is one other thing that I perhaps shouldn't even bring up, but you seem to be a very intelligent woman and I think you could see the rationale behind it," he began, then hesitated. His inner conflict about how to broach this possibly forbidden topic was painfully obvious, and I grew fearful of what he might tell me next. After all that had happened and that he told me already, what possibly could I find surprising anymore? A small nod and release of a held breath told me that he had made up his mind about something, and so he resumed from where he left off. "When the community is endangered and we need to make a fast break from here—a clean getaway—in search of a new home, it is sometimes necessary to destroy some or all of the Dingoes in the packs. This of course depends on a number of factors, principal among these being what time of the month it is, how many and how well-behaved they are, if there will be someone to look after them—as we don't want any getting out into the wild, returning to wreak havoc on a human town and announcing our existence before our two species are ready for it. It basically all depends on our ability to keep and protect them on top of caring for our own under emergency conditions."

"Great, more euthanizing," I quipped weakly, all the wind knocked out of my sail, so that I literally deflated into a slump where I sat.

"Listen," he said, attempting to console me, "don't you worry about that, you hear? Now I have something even more important to address, and I think it's probably the most important topic we need to discuss tonight."

"And that is?" I asked blankly, looking up at him with little interest or enthusiasm.

"Sex."

Yes, that's right; I heard him correctly. He said "sex." "Excuse me?" is what I said in response, but not until I stared at him for perhaps a good twenty seconds.

"It's bound to happen. I know of very few who abstain completely, and certainly none from this community. But the most important thing is that you know the golden rule."

"And that is?" I asked, still recovering from this new twist in the direction our conversation took.

"No Dingo may have intercourse with another Dingo. The product of such a union would be *another* Dingo, and we do not want to increase their numbers. It's a simple rule, and you probably already see the sense behind it. I'm sure you wouldn't want to bring a child into this world knowing what he will have to endure, so this shouldn't be a problem."

"Then what *is* the problem," I asked, thinking myself very astute to realize that there was more he wasn't yet telling me. He seemed impressed by my intuitiveness as well.

"Well, quite frankly," he began, and I think he might have been blushing. Was this the same man who sniffed my crotch and howled at the moon? "You may eventually... find that you need... that your desires become over—" He took a breath and, sensing my amusement at his discomfort, and no doubt getting enraged over it, he began again, more like the Jack I knew. "You may get horny, sister, and then whatta ya gonna do about it? Huh?" I though he was being rhetorical, but he was actually waiting for my answer.

"Don't worry, I've spent plenty of time without and can survive it," I said, not at all wanting to discuss my intentions with him. I then thought to myself just what my intentions would be, and realized I did not have a clue. The thought of giving up sex entirely... well that was about as bad as anything else that had happened to me that night or that had been addressed so far. I needed to know my options. Thankfully, Jack knew that already and offered them to me without forcing me to endure the ignominiousness of asking.

"First of all, your drive will probably peter off a bit, as you will only be in heat once a year."

Disbelieving, I asked him to clarify: "You mean I'm only going to get my period..."

"Once a year, yes. Ya see, there is a silver lining. Women always love that part the best. Anyway, the downside is that, during that time of the year, your desire *will be* quite intense."

That time of the year, I thought, thinking that it had a nice ring to it. No more "that time of the month" but "that time of the year." I think I actually swooned. Then I realized he was saying things that I definitely needed to hear.

"And you can have sex all you want with my breed because we're not compatible; we can't get you pregnant."

"Yes," I recalled, "the Professor told me as much, but I didn't believe him."

"Well you can believe it. The only ones who can impregnate you are humans. And other Dingoes, of course. But I've already warned you of the outcome of such a union. If you *must* have sex, it *must* be with one of us. Oh, and uh... there's one thing I should inform you about that. In all things, my kind prefers to be in their natural form. Sex is no exception."

Wait a minute. "So if I want to have sex..."

"It will have to be with a *Canis sapien* in wolf form," he finished my thought for me.

"That's bestiality," I uttered without thinking. I'm sure my remark must have been offensive to him but he did not show it. Perhaps he's used to this reaction.

"You may find someone who's willing to perform as a human; it's not unheard of. But don't expect that nicety from most of us."

"I wouldn't mind as much if I could be in that form as well, but the only time I will even be close to that is when the moon is full, and when that happens I'll..."

"Yes, you'll be sedated. Otherwise you'd be too wild and uncontrollable even for the most sexually experimental of our kind," he chuckled.

My cheeks flushed. And then what he said next affronted and angered me further.

"If you're interested, I'd be willing to try it your way, as a favor and to make it up to you for doing all this to you in the first place."

My reply came without even having to think about it. "I'd rather chew off my own foot."

This time he was visibly offended. "Fine," he snapped at me, and moved toward the tent flap. "Then you know your other option. I suggest you be *open* to the experience," he added leeringly. Before exiting, he stopped to ask me one thing more. "Why is it that you hate me so much? Because of what happened to the old dog? Or because of what happened to you?"

I didn't have an answer for him, and so he slipped out into the cool night. The awful howling outside filled the tent and made me painfully aware of my situation. I was doomed.

FOUR

I don't know how, but at some point I actually fell asleep that night. There had been a fresh supply of tampons provided for me, which I availed myself of thankfully, and so to some extent I was made a bit more comfortable physically. Emotionally was another story.

I dreamt of a fancy restaurant, one from my imagination only and that I had never been to. An elegant-looking, smartly dressed maitre-d' approached a table where a couple sat down. But although they were dressed normally and sat upright like everyone else in the fine establishment, I suddenly saw that they were dogs sitting at the table. But the maitre-d' and the rest of the patrons took no notice as the pair was served an elaborate feast and began to eat, with knife and fork and napkins folded daintily in their laps!

The maitre-d' seemed pleased, and then turned to the rest of his customers and presented a small gong, which he proceeded to strike like a dinner bell. At once the human diners lunged forward and tore into the food on their plates, using their teeth to tear and rend the flesh of their dinner servings. I awoke with a start, and saw that it was morning outside. I had made it through my first night in the camp.

• • • • •

"Jack's busy, so I'll be giving you your tour of the town today."

There she was, my bitter enemy, staring me in the face with her usual open arrogance. At least Jack put on a show of concern for me; this woman was an icicle. I don't know why I hated Aryana so much, infinitely more than Jack himself in fact. She acted threatening to me—who posed no threat to her whatsoever—for absolutely no reason, and that must have mainly been why I felt as strongly as I did. All I knew was that I was going to have to parade around town with her as my escort-guide, and that if she wanted to she could tear out my throat without the slightest bit of resistance on my part. I was in her hands.

"In this pack, you can think of Jack, its alpha, as your president. I, being the alpha's bitch, am the equivalent of 'first lady.' I have power without having to participate in any power struggle, and if someone were to usurp the alpha position, I would go along with the title as the new alpha's bitch."

"I thought wolves mated for life," I said, recalling hearing that tidbit in a film that probably my brother had watched.

"Maybe true wolves do, and maybe they don't. We try, just as you do, but we have the same issues plaguing our relationships as your species does, things our brothers in nature couldn't possibly comprehend and certainly don't have to worry themselves about."

"So what if the new alpha doesn't want you?" I said, feeling ballsy but hoping that she didn't take it as a personal affront. It was, after all, a fair question.

She turned to me, perhaps deciding how to respond, perhaps deciding whether to rip out my lungs for a snack, then turned and answered matter-of-factly, "Then I would join Jack, if he still wanted me. Our pack is too small to bother with petty jealousies and such. Even our bids for power and position are more social and intellectual, not just two wolves going at it like in the wild. Although there is a bit of that too, as our leader *has* to be in a position to present himself as the finest our pack has to offer, especially in dealings with other packs and pack leaders. But it's more about determining the best choice for the role, not simply posturing."

Funny she should put it that way, as I found that most of her behavior, at least toward me so far, was nothing but pointless posturing, plain and simple.

We stepped out of my tent, which was on the isolated outskirts of the community, and approached the cabins and lodges of the town proper. There were many people outside, enjoying many of the things that outdoor life has to offer, and although I was a stranger intruding upon their lifestyle, they paid no heed to my presence at all. An attractive mother sat on a wooden bench nursing her baby with breast fully revealed, showing no concern at all about her exposure. And no one else paid her any mind either—except for me, that is. I had stopped and stared embarrassingly with open mouth, and later I felt ashamed for my behavior, but at the time I felt I was justified in my stupefaction. The babe she was nursing was a wolf pup. Sure it was hers, and sure I had been told that they were born in their true form, so naturally a baby would not know how to assume a human guise, but the sight of a human-looking woman with an animal suckling at her breast in the middle of day in the bright outdoors was more culture shock then I was prepared for.

Aryana roughly shoved me along in front of her and turned to make some gesture of apology to the woman. But I didn't see this. I was too busy looking at the children running around, playing in the dirt. We were walking through their play area, and I was suddenly deathly afraid that one or all of them would suddenly transform and lunge at me, just for the sheer pleasure of scaring the new girl.

But none of them even took notice of us, and once we were passed them we approached a two-story tavern with some more human-looking women, only these were watching us intently from where they leaned out the windows of the second floor. We stopped in front of it, and I felt uncomfortable under the scrutiny of these women and wondered why Aryana had stopped here.

"You haven't given any thoughts yet as to what function you'd like to play in our little community, have you?" she asked, and I detected a subtle smirk in her expression that was reflected in her tone.

"Well what positions are open?" I carefully queried, feeling uncomfortable about this whole tour and expecting her to play me for a fool any chance she could get.

"You see those women?" she said, nodding her head up at our audience in the balcony. I nodded expectantly. "They're Dingoes just like you. Chose to offer their services to delight and satisfy the wanton men in our community with their bald, puny bodies and their lackluster skills," she said in disdain. She snapped her head up at them sharply, and they all fled from the windows in an instant. So I wasn't the only one who feared the gaze of this female. Or was it just that all Dingoes fear the natural supremacy of their *Canis sapien* masters?

Aryana turned back to me, a smile of amusement on her full lips. "No, I see you as more of a teacher-type, is that right? One more suited to using her brains than her body."

Where the hell did she get off...? I was infuriated by the insinuation, but didn't know how to retaliate. I mean, she was right in that I'd rather teach than prostitute myself, but how do I defend my sexual ability without sounding like I was extolling the virtues of being a slut? "Yes, I might enjoy teaching," I remarked, "but maybe I could teach those girls in the arts of lovemaking if they're as lacking as you say." It was a weak retort, but the best I could do under the circumstances. I felt like an idiot and was right about one thing. She *was* out to make me look foolish any chance she could get.

"Had much experience pleasing canines, have you?" she said, with that now-all-too-familiar leer back on her face. "Little late-night action with Fluffy back in your experimental days in college, perhaps? You have heard about that, haven't you? How we prefer to *do it* 'in the fur'?"

My face must have flushed, for she seemed satisfied with the reaction she provoked. Then I had a brainstorm. My cheeks glowed for a different reason as I looked her in the eye and mentioned how Jack offered to oblige in human form out of consideration for me. *That* ruffled her feathers. Suddenly suspecting a possible cause for her belligerence toward me, I pressed my advantage with a query as to whether Jack frequently reassigns the role of pack bitch.

She shot forward till she was but inches in front of me, a snarl rumbling from behind teeth that had lengthened to fangs as she fought to control herself from biting a piece out of me. Her breath came in short, quick exhalations, and she said between breaths, "No matter *who* the alpha takes as the pack bitch, you can guarantee that it will NEVER... be a Dingo."

I toyed with the thought of correcting her grammar—"No matter *whom*"—but thought better of it. Getting a rise out of her was one thing; provoking her to resort to her natural instincts and kill me was another. I decided to quit while I was ahead. "What kind of teachers do you need?"

Changing the subject seemed to work. She seemed momentarily distracted, like a confused animal, then gathered herself together and explained their unique schooling requirements to me. It wasn't help in the regular courses that concerned them; anything that they could learn in a book was no problem for them. Their teachers went over such things, of course, but much of that material was covered in the individual homes. The area that they needed the most work in was in acting human. And that's where Dingoes came in especially handy, and why it isn't frowned upon too heavily to occasionally bring a new one into the fold. Keeping up-to-date with current trends and behavioral idiosyncrasies—things not really touched upon in TV news coverages—were the things that they wanted to learn how to nail perfectly.

As she explained, the reason why most of them will be found walking around on two legs instead of four during the daytime was because they are constantly alert to the fact that at any given moment they may be under surveillance by some satellite or government camera operating out of one of those notorious "black helicopters" made popular by conspiracy theorists, who seem to have some fears in common with this folk. And so acting as normal as possible, by our standards, is of crucial importance to them. They try not to alter their lifestyle completely though, and they allow—no, they actually encourage—their young to change forms at will and learn to become comfortable in either one. Despite their need to practice holding human form and acting like one, great value is placed on recreation and running free in their natural form. Many of their youngsters, as is the case with my own people, are seduced by TV and video games, and there is actually a tendency among them to stay in human form—to *fit in* with the modern world—until puberty hits and their natural drives kick in more. When I mentioned the children we had passed and how they weren't in school, I learned that although education was deemed important, so was running and playing, the canine way of life.

Another obvious reason for possessing human form as much as possible, aside from the practice excuse, was that the developments that they reside in were always manmade and designed for the human form. Doorknobs, drawers, chairs, etc. Everything was easier to manipulate with hands and feet. Paws may have their superiority out on the naked earth, but in man's dwellings they were insufficient to the tasks at hand, no pun intended.

Perhaps of greater importance was the desire to be so convincing as a human that they could infiltrate our society in order to obtain information needed by the community. In addition to medical and scientific knowledge, *Canis sapiens* needed to bring back warnings when a community was going to be investigated because the legitimate landowners have discovered their property being used without their approval. The grounds they currently inhabited were lost in the shuffle during an acquisition/change of power between two land development corporations, and a use for it will no doubt be determined when the oversight is eventually noted. They often inhabit woodland areas before companies get around to their plans for deforestation, with the trees being turned into lumber and furniture, a fate offensive to their nature-loving ideology. Aryana also dropped a hint that their best human impersonators end up as plants among political parties and government facilities, and she heavily implied that organizations like the FBI provided their best opportunities for information retrieval. They apparently had an "early warning system" to rival our own military's.

I remarked that the Professor mentioned their inability to obtain proper employment, to which Aryana attempted to skirt the subject. When I pressed further on this, she enlightened me with the knowledge that occasionally they manage to find someone who dies young and looks similar enough to one of their own, providing the rare opportunity for one of their kind to slip into their shoes. I realized what type of person she might mean, someone either without a family or outcast by them, a drug addict most likely, whose inevitable early demise might go unnoticed for weeks before discovery. Someone whose body could be removed without instant revelation, and whose identification — and identity — could be usurped with the right measures taken. Obviously the identity swap would only work far from their original home — another state, most likely — removing as much as possible the threat of being recognized as a fraud. But since someone with a record would not be a candidate for the FBI, the person they would need would have to be quite young. It saddened me to think about the poor soul who would fit their requirements, and saddened me further to realize that they were probably not as hard to find as one might imagine.

"Okay, so let's get you acquainted with your new boss," she said, and then proceeded to enter the tavern in front of us, which I already knew to be a brothel. I didn't know whether she was joking, or perhaps cruel enough to try to force me into a profession I did not want to engage in, but then she poked her head back outside and said to me, "C'mon. The madam of this house is also the school principal."

I thought of making some crack about the sort of double-major she must have had in college, but as I stepped through the door into the cathouse I lost the ability to speak, or at least to be smug. Inside, arrayed on barstools and reclining chairs that surrounded a card table, a piano, or a bar where a young woman served drinks, were the burly macho types I had seen with Aryana in the pickup truck. I didn't know if they were the same exact individuals, but they all had that same rugged, woodsy, outdoor look like the ones that were accomplices to the Professor's murder last night. And they all had that same look in their eyes, like they were famished animals... and I was a slab of meat.

Aryana looked around at them and noticed how some were sniffing at the air around them, as if they were sampling my scent from afar to see how I might taste. She turned to me, glanced down, and inhaled deeply. "Damn," she muttered beneath her breath. "That hasn't stopped yet, has it. No, I guess it wouldn't—too soon and all."

She was speaking more to herself, but I understood what she was referring to and recognized the dangerous situation I might suddenly be in. To these horny men—and I use the term loosely, as they are not really *men*—a bitch in heat just sauntered in, and this *was* after all the right place for what they were obviously craving. So what would be my excuse not to sympathize and deliver? I was too dumbstruck to think of a way out of this mess, but fortunately Aryana was on my side for once. She put herself between me and my admirers, and I could detect a warning growl emitting from her throat. She had possessed such an air of authority over the masculine pack members the night before, but I didn't know just how high-ranking the alpha's bitch really was, or if their engaged sex drives might factor in to whether they respected that authority under these conditions.

I prayed that Aryana would whisk me away to whatever part of the house this madam was in and quickly, but before we could retreat toward any exit a woman who was obviously in charge here entered, leaving us with no choice but to remain where we stood. She shot a dirty look at her customers, some of whom had risen from their stools and stepped tentatively toward us, and then approached me with her hands up as if greeting a long-lost dear friend, appraising me up and down as if seeing how time had changed me. I realized, of course, what she was appraising me for and why, but I was too grateful for her presence to act indignant toward her and ruin what could possibly be a very good friendship. She would also make a powerful ally in this community. A woman in her forties or possibly a well-preserved fifties, she was plump but not unpleasantly so, her curves speaking volumes about the pleasures she could provide in her own place of business—*if* she were an active participant and not just its proprietor, that is.

She glanced briefly at Aryana, and then resumed checking me over. "Is she, uh...?"

"Working for you, yes," Aryana answered. "But not here; over at the school."

The joyous expression fell from the madam's face, as she said to me, without hiding her disappointment: "All *that,* and not put to good use! Well that's just a shame. Perhaps you don't realize just how noble and important a service you would be providing here. The average male in this community gets a sexual urge eight to ten times a day; the average female gets one once a year..."

I glanced over at Aryana in disbelief, and she gave a quick, furtive shake of her head as if to say "Don't you believe it!"

The madam either didn't notice or didn't deign to acknowledge Aryana's gesture, and went on lecturing without missing a beat. "So what do you think keeps these ravenous beasts from going hog-wild and engaging in some killing spree? Us! That's what! Provide them with something they can sink their teeth into—" She must have seen the sudden look of horror on my face because she added: "Figuratively speaking, of course! Give them an outlet for their passions and they won't seek it elsewhere—like in your hometown! What would you rather have, a community of contented townsfolk or a pack of deprived wolves, seeking relief from their desires and strong enough to have their way with the majority of this world's inhabitants?"

I stood quietly gaping, and then Aryana again came to my aid by remarking, "You know, Jezebel, I never get tired of hearing your sales pitch. I can't imagine why more of our newcomers don't join you immediately upon hearing it."

Jezebel, if that was her real name, didn't appreciate the sarcasm, but simply swallowed back whatever retort she obviously was about to unleash upon Aryana and just asked her if I'd seen the school yet. As Aryana started to reply, a slight movement caught her eye, interrupting her, and a second later I felt an intensely warm sensation high on the back of my thighs and the bottom curves of my butt cheeks. My skirt was sticky and clinging to my skin, and it only took me another second to realize that it was not because of me or my period, but that one of the more brazen patrons of this establishment had snuck up behind me, pants down to his knees, and was "marking his territory" on my behind!

Jezebel began bawling him out, trying to lure him away from me by offering him immediate access to one of the ready enticements waiting for him upstairs, when Aryana stepped in to handle things more decisively. He was a huge, muscular man in his thirties, but the yelp that suddenly came from him would have been more appropriate coming from... well, from me!

I saw Aryana's head from where I now stood behind the man, but only part of her face was visible between his legs. The man's body was blocking most of it from my angle, but I was able to tell that she had a firm grip on his testicles between her teeth—or rather, her fangs. The stream had stopped, and the man was slowly crouching over, suffering but afraid to move for fear of eliciting more pain. He eventually made it all the way to the ground, and lay with his back to the floor and his knees up, whimpering plaintively. Aryana finally removed her mouth from his privates and crouched over the man, having to hike her dress up nearly to her hips in order to spread her legs wide enough to straddle him. The man beneath her faced away from her with his neck slightly lifted. I realized with a start that he was offering his throat to her, an act of submission I had heard about among dogs.

Aryana was still hunched over him, snarling silently and poised threateningly, and I and everyone in the place—perhaps Aryana herself—wondered what she was going to do to the offender. Jezebel took a bold step forward and said "Aryana."

Aryana looked up, and then back down at the man, who was still faced away from her. She reached out for Jezebel to give her a hand up, and as she stood with a foot at either side of the man's head, she let loose with a stream of her own right onto the man's shamed face. This was apparently a great dishonor, and most of the men turned away rather than serve in humiliating him further. He was obviously one of their friends, and a favorite among them, and they didn't want to add to his insult.

"Take her to room 5; there's a bathroom and closet in there. After she cleans up, give her whatever clothes there fit her," Jezebel told Aryana, and as we left the charged atmosphere of the room, I could hear the proprietor working to clear the air and set everything right again.

In room 5 I stripped in front of Aryana, less conscious of how my naked body looked than I was eager to rid myself of the tainted clothes from my skin. I realized that I owed a lot to her and with difficulty I quietly spoke the words "Thank you." She graciously ignored my words and didn't gloat like I had feared, but she did stare at my body as I exposed more and more of myself, which naturally made me uncomfortable. A smile of amusement crept onto her face, and I wondered what part of me she had found so funny, but it was my panties that she thought of as comical, and she commented on how no one in the community ever bothers to wear them.

As she opened the bathroom door, went in, and ran the water for my bath, I realized that this explained how she was able to easily pee in that man's face without moving aside underwear, something that I noted subliminally but could not devote any thought to at the time. After a few minutes she waved me in, having adjusted the water to what she thought was a tolerable temperature, and as I stepped past her and tested it for myself with my foot, she went on to explain the reason for their choice of dress. "You see, clothing is an inhibitor in the act of transforming back to our true form. We don't like to wear it, we don't think it's natural to wear it, and we choose to wear as little of it as possible. Underwear is simply unnecessary. As for nudity, we see each other naked all the time in our natural state, so I guess you can think of us as being European in our approach to the human body. Except that most of us don't think much of the *human* body; we find our canine forms much more sexually attractive."

I had found the water temperature to be to my pleasing and was soaking comfortably in her presence, feeling less uncomfortable about her watching me bathe after this latest admission. And I figured that the sex-symbol attention I rated upon first entering this establishment was entirely due to the odor I gave off, and not because they found me so irresistibly desirable—a slight blow to my ego, I must admit. In a moment of unguarded comfort and relaxation, I told this to Aryana, and she smiled in a sisterly way.

Since we were being so friendly to each other—which I decided not to read too much into, as she may have simply been told to act this way to make my transition into this new lifestyle easier—I leaned back and asked what they would do if I ever escaped. I was aware that such a question would reveal my intent to try to sneak away when the opportunity arose, but I figured that every newcomer entertained such a desire during their first days in the camp, and that they wouldn't find it out of the ordinary for me to ask this.

"That wouldn't be wise," Aryana replied, and as I expected she was not surprised or put off in the slightest by my question. "You need us. No one out there can help you; no one has any experience with this."

"I could try a doctor, or a scientist. One of them might—"

"Help you?" she interrupted, finishing my own sentence but turning it into a question. "No. Oh, they'd love to get their hands on you though. Stick you in a room, pump you full of tranquilizers, and study you during the full moon. Cut off parts of your body and watch you regenerate. Take blood and skin samples and try to adapt this ability for themselves. At the very least, you'd become a sideshow freak, fodder for the dirt rags and daytime talk show circuits."

"Surely..." I began, but not as confidently as I'd wished to be. "Some must have escaped before?" I continued, inadvertently turning it into a question.

"I've heard things," she replied vaguely. "All packs have their tales about 'the one that got away,' telling all kinds of stories about what happened to the fugitives. Canine urban legends. You never know what to believe. We had an escapee when I was young. All types of fates were predicted for him. Well, regardless of what the community decided had happened to him, me and some other pups found what was left of the body while exploring in the woods. He'd been hunted down and shot full of silver. But no matter what we said, the pack generated its own myth. The other pups heard it and embellished it with their own exaggerated or flat-out invented details, and — voila! — instant legend."

"Okay, so don't expect help from out there," I summarized. "And what can I expect from the community?"

"Jack's already explained all that, I'm sure," Aryana said with a sigh, looking suddenly tired. It must be a subject that she's weary of explaining, for she suddenly got defensive about it. "Look, it's an unfortunate event, but you brought it on yourself. He gave you plenty of chances to walk away and just *go home*."

"And he would've let me?" I asked, sounding more than a bit skeptical. "After all that I had already learned?"

"Yes!" she said, wholeheartedly devout in her belief in her mate. In her alpha. "With what you had, you could concoct a clever comic book; nothing more."

This was utterly pointless. She would support her leader as one would a king or president, with the devotion of a veteran or patriot. I wanted to enjoy my bath, so I sought out a more agreeable topic of conversation, and one which could provide me information I could use. "So how far could I expect to go here, being a Dingo and all? Jezebel seems to have done all right for herself, being both a school principle *and* madam of one of the town's more prosperous businesses, from the looks of things."

"Is your nose purely there for ornamentation?" she asked me in disgust. "Jezebel's not a Dingo. Can't you smell the difference between our kinds yet?" I didn't have a chance to answer, as she added: "And secondly, this may be a busy place, but it is *not* a prosperous one. We don't use money here. I thought that would've already been explained to you."

"It was. I guess it's one of the hardest things to accept." Whatever bond we may have been developing before was a distant memory, as she was once again treating me as she had the night before, like an inferior being. I tried some levity again, hoping to bring back a little of the goodwill between us. "I can accept a tribe of wolves that transform into men, but the concept of a community that doesn't rely on money is just too farfetched." It didn't work; her newly returned cold attitude remained frozen in place. She looked down at the bathwater and suggested I get out before the water turns completely red and my bathing will have been for nothing.

I looked down at the small cloud of blood that seemed to offend her somehow and decided that my bath was indeed over. As I rose, I made an observation. "If you don't wear underwear, whatta you do when you're in heat?"

"Spend most of our time as wolves, licking ourselves as needed. You Dingoes can't do that though, since you can only change when it's beyond your control, so you'll probably choose to dress as you're accustomed. And some of us even try some of your hygiene products when we have to be in human form for a long-enough time period, but it's never without discomfort."

"Be glad you've only had to endure it once a year all your life," I muttered as I dried myself off with the towel Aryana tossed at me before going to the closet Jezebel mentioned and opening it for my inspection.

Before joining her at the closet I took a gamble and opened one of the drawers of a small chest beside the room's bed. To my satisfaction I found what I had hoped for, underwear, douches, and tampons. The prostitutes were, after all, formerly humans, and not natural *Canis sapiens*. I retreated to the bathroom, but Aryana followed me to watch as I cleaned up. I wasn't pleased about this, but didn't say anything. She seemed so curious, like an inexperienced child observing her mother for the first time to learn how to do it herself. When I had hiked up my new panties — not finding a brassiere, and doubting that these women would ever bother with one — I went to the closet to check sizes and make my selection.

The dresses were all in the style that seemed to be the prerequisite in this community, simple and easily removable, yet with a sexiness that obviously stems from the ready accessibility they offer. Aryana and every other female I'd seen here so far all dressed as if they could slip out of their clothes in a second's notice. The prostitutes' apparel was no more extravagant than that, and nothing as exotic or sheer as our own prostitutes are known to wear. But then if Aryana is right and they don't find us terribly attractive in human form to begin with, then sex appeal isn't an issue anyway, and there would be no need to dress to impress. All they had to do was go down on all fours naked... and not really do anything else. So I imagine. One thing's for sure: I was not eager to find out. Perhaps celibacy *would* be an option I could live with, given the alternative.

I picked out a powder blue dress that happened to catch my eye; it had a lacy white trim at collar and cuffs, and a faintly perceived floral pattern that was nearly invisible but subtly made itself known. Aryana made a quick nod and said, "Perfect school teacher outfit." All was apparently right with the world; we were somehow back to hating each other.

When we returned to the scene of the offense, there were less men lingering about—most notably, my arrogant assailant was no longer there—thank God—probably off in some suite getting his issues resolved while engaged in an act of bestiality. How did those women do it? "The girls who work here, are they all Dingoes or are some like you and Jezebel?" I asked Aryana as we walked out the door.

"Be serious. Why would any of my kind have to degrade herself by working there?" she replied, keeping true to form by answering me in a way that managed to stick an insult in. "And Jezebel only keeps things running, like she does at the school, just because she's good at running things; that's her talent. She doesn't do anything else, if that's what you're wondering. Pleasing horny males that just gotta mate all the damn time is not part of our daily duties. Them's Dingo work," she added with a mock Western accent, making me realize what this town reminded me of. As we walked along the dirt roads amidst the plain wood buildings, I got a definite sense of being in The Old West, right down to its people and establishments. The brothel, the card tables by the piano and bar, the grungy, earthy cowboy types—albeit updated to an almost-Harley Davidson biker look. And the innocent newly arrived school teacher of a school with no legitimate (or matriculating) education system.

We arrived at the school, which to my disappointment was a building just like all the rest, except that it had a playground-type schoolyard area in front, with an unusual pen that held no animals at the moment. I had gotten lost in my musings that I had almost expected (and even actually looked forward) to find the school to be one of those cliché red buildings that were around in the old days.

"No need to go inside and disturb any class that might still be in session. Just show up tomorrow morning before six and see Jezebel, who'll be inside waiting for ya."

"Six?"

"Yeah, we like to do things real early, around here. 'Up with the chickens' sorta thing. Since we're usually up all night doing wolfy things, and since midday is the time when people get all run down to the ground, we sleep then. Noon to us is like midnight to your people. To be truthful I don't know why you don't keep similar schedules. I've heard how people in offices start noddin' off after their lunch hour. Think about it. The sun's beatin' down full, you've just filled your belly; what would make the most sense just then but going to sleep? Your culture's all backward when it comes to that. Just 'cause the sun's down don't mean you gotta stop livin'. Especially once you discovered your own means of providing light and electricity. You can make it daytime any time you want, and yet you still stick to that same old routine like the world would come to an end if you went to sleep while the sun was still up."

As I looked about at the bustling activity in these still-early hours, I couldn't help but admit that there was something to this sort of schedule. Adapting to these new hours might be the easiest part about my reconditioning. We had walked past the school, and from her purposeful stride I assumed there was something else she had to show me; her walk was not casual enough for this to just be a stroll. A grumble from my stomach reminded me that I hadn't eaten anything since that bag of grapes that I brought along for the ride yesterday evening, and I hoped she was taking me someplace where we could get some food.

We stopped at a cabin, which didn't look at all like a town eatery, and she explained that this was where I would sleep and keep my things. My new home. Having spent the past night like a pariah on the outskirts of the community, I was surprised that it was so centrally located, practically in the middle of the town itself. I voiced this thought to her.

"Of course you're in the middle. *Surrounded,* as it were. Last night we just didn't want you to interact with anyone until you were ready. But we have to keep all Dingoes centrally located for everyone's protection, you see. You'll not only be sleeping there, but you'll be chained in there as well when the moon is full, and drugged so you don't rip off a limb trying to get out. If you did get out, you'd have to go through all of us before getting to the woods, and that buys us some time, because once you're in the woods it makes hunting you down more difficult. Not impossible—hardly! We have scent trackers that put to shame those lazy bloodhounds of yours. But difficult nevertheless because time will be against us. And if we have to pursue you to a village beyond the forests... well, depending on whether you come into contact with anyone, there may be some messy cleanup involved, with trying to hide bodies and destroy evidence, or make it look like something else happened. Although trying to make a wolf attack look like something less primal and more an aspect of your world—like a gang slaying, for instance, or some cult sacrifice—isn't exactly the easiest thing to accomplish.

"And again, that's another thing your instructions will be helpful in, keeping us abreast of the latest vices and crimes so that, if needed, we could better pull off such a misdirection in regards to our own necessary forays into your world. As much as we hate to admit it, we often need things from your people to survive—"

"I know," I interrupted, "medicines and stuff. The scavenger way of life and all."

"Right," she continued. "But after we've done what we had to do, it's important to make it look like someone *else* had been there, for any other purpose your investigators will buy. And that's why reporters like yourself make the best new additions to our world. You've seen and reported on such events and know the score. But unlike, let's say, a cop, you won't have the training—or even the balls—to constantly fight or resist us, and thus make conditioning you such a problem."

Well I wasn't about to enlighten her on the very limited and unimpressive background of experience I had thus far enjoyed in my journalistic career, but as for secretly keeping the fight alive and never giving up hope that I would someday get out of here and back to my old life, I'd show her who had balls. I recalled the silver earrings back among my things in the tent, and found comfort in the fact that I could kill her in her sleep—if I could just sneak up on her without her hearing or smelling me.

That last thought came to me in such a natural way that I amazed myself. There must have been some change going on in me all right, for I have never thought about taking another's life in so casual a manner. And here I was, actually taking *comfort* in the knowledge that I could kill someone... Well that just wasn't me! And if that was any indication of what sort of being I was to become, then I didn't like the way this was going at all.

Aryana suddenly turned and watched as a man, still a long way off, headed in our direction. She seemed to know that he was heading toward us. She turned to me and informed me: "There'll be a Hyena arriving today that'll entertain us tonight, but since the moon's still full you won't be able to join in. Shame. Their visits are few and far between, and they are definitely worth seeing. Another day or so and you won't have to worry about the moon arousing your cravings. You might even get away with going this whole cycle without a transformation. That'll be lucky for you, and more importantly it'll give the rest of us a break."

"Wait, back up. There are *were-hyenas* too?"

She smiled, but I was no longer warmed by her smiles. That period was brief and gone, and her smiles to me were once again cause for fueling my distaste of her. "No, he's not a real hyena. That's just what we call those of us who travel across the land, bringing stories and updates of major events happening in the other communities."

"I see, *slang*. And here I would've thought a Hyena was a stand-up comic."

"They often are. When telling stories, they like to keep us entertained. They're respected individuals who belong to no *one* pack, but to the species as a whole. They have a talent for being informative in an entertaining, storyteller fashion, and they do so around a campfire at night, just like in the old traditional way. Just like in your traditions too."

Interesting. I was sorry I was going to miss this delightful-sounding diversion.

"We have other slang terms that are similar to yours: a 'Fox' being a sly, crafty person; a 'Jackal' being wicked or a scoundrel. Those horny bastards back at Jezebel's I would call 'Coyotes.' That's the term for those of us who like humans a bit too much."

"What about 'Feline'?" I offered. "Do you use that or any other cat reference as an insult to each other?"

"Yes, that would work as an insult," she said, and then sneered and added as she turned to the man who had reached us by then: "So would 'Human.'"

"Jack sent me to ask you to oversee preparations for tonight's big event," the newcomer informed her. "You're needed in back of the Social Center."

"I expected as much," she replied to him wearily. Then a sudden gleam in her eye set her crooked smile into play again, and she gave me a sidelong glance as she said to him, "I trust you can take over Beverly's indoctrination for the rest of the day."

He smiled and nodded all too willingly, and I wondered what she was getting me into now. As he sidled up alongside me, she walked away, adding almost as an afterthought: "After all, it wasn't that long ago since you had yours."

I look at him anew—actually I hadn't fully looked at him at all until then, for I was afraid of what he might want with me. "You're a... a Dingo?" I asked hesitantly, and a bit hopefully, but mostly afraid I might be insulting him if I misunderstood Aryana's comment.

"Yes, going on six months now," he answered pleasantly, not at all bitter or resentful about it as I would have expected from someone here for half a year. "Bill Jensen," he declared, holding out his hand and giving me a warm handshake. Now that I knew he wasn't one of *them*, and thus not part of last night's events, I considered him frankly and decided that he was very attractive. He kept his brown hair short but not too short, suggesting that he may have worked in an office setting before all this, and he was taller than me and in decent shape, his age perhaps falling in the thirties.

"Beverly Journal," I announced, delighted to be speaking with someone of my species. You'd think I had not seen another human for days the way I practically gushed!

"Yes, I know. We have the same initials."

"Oh please," I said. "I hate my name, but my initials are even worse. Do you know how much teasing I received in high school over them?" I don't know why I shared this personal detail, except that I was desperate for an ally among this group, and a handsome one would be even nicer. Thus I was doomed to embarrass myself before him — at least I hadn't made the 'I can't wait to get married so I can change my last name' remark that I always seem to have to insert somewhere, both in apology for my name (as if it were something I should be ashamed of) and to show that I had a sense of humor about it (which I really didn't).

"BJ," he said, trying it out for size. "I like that. Mind if I call you that?"

The answer should have been obvious, but then I surprised myself by saying, "Well, okay. But only because you're one too." First the Professor, and now him. At least I didn't act this way around Jack.

"I'll bet you're hungry," he ventured, and my stomach suddenly let out a response so that I wouldn't have to. Perhaps it was afraid I'd put my foot in my mouth some more and blow any chances it had of getting filled today. "I'll take that as a yes," he joked. "These people forget that we don't follow their way of life in all regards. We don't forage and attack in the wild; we don't eat as if meals were some afterthought, picking a snack here and there as part of our daily routine. A squirrel here, a chipmunk there, and—'ooh, there's a plump little raccoon. I'll race ya to see who gets him first!'" I giggled at his mimicking of their mentality, but my stomach was insisting he get on with it. "C'mon. We Dingoes, and many of *them* too, take our meals at the Social Center."

"You've mentioned that place before," I remarked as he led the way. "That's where Aryana went."

"Well don't worry about her. She'll be behind the building, setting up in the campground where they'll be listening to their Hyena guest tonight."

"I'm not worried," I said, unconvincingly trying to act like she didn't bother me at all. "What makes you think that?"

"Well she has a way of strutting around here like she owns the place, making people feel small in the process. Dingoes especially."

"Whew, so it's not just me," I uttered, instantly blowing my charade of unconcern toward her.

He laughed. "No, it's not just you. And it's not just Dingoes. Anyway, not all *Canis sapiens* are like her and Jack. In fact, like us, no too are entirely alike in personality. They try to make it seem like they got it all together and are 'at one communing with nature' and all that, but they've got the same problems as us. Well, not the *same* problems, but *as many* problems as us. Plus they're always on the run, worried about extinction and discovery." His voice trailed off, and I got the impression that he sympathized with them.

"You... don't seem to mind what they did to you. You sound like you like it here among them."

"Oh, I do! Back in the world, I wrote for a newspaper. Can you imagine what all this newsworthy stuff means to me? Oh, wait, of course you do. You're one too; I almost forgot. The stories of each Dingo here and what happened to them; the revelation of a race as old as ours that's been kept hidden from us all these years, complete with its own culture, society, rules. I'm fascinated every day with some new tidbit of information I can garner from somewhere. There's enough here to fill a book."

Okay, that discouraged me. Here I thought I was the one with the great idea, and then Mr. Reporter (who I had automatically concluded was so much more talented and experienced than me) had six months of digging and research over me. I was disheartened.

"Here we are," he announced, leading me inside a building that looked just like any other here, except that it was perhaps longer than the rest. "In here, members from all the five packs mingle and enjoy human cuisine or watch television—if the pups aren't hogging it as usual. There are pool tables and Ping-Pong tables, a swimming pool—*they* prefer natural ponds, however. And a cafeteria with the best Dingo cook in the community—oh, yeah, right, she's the *only* Dingo cook in the community. But her cooking's not bad, and she's easy on the eyes—" He caught himself and sheepishly added, "But you're probably not interested in that bit of information." He looked at me out of the corner of his eyes and asked "Or are you?"

I could tell that he was interested in learning my sexual orientation, and decided to tease him awhile by not answering with anything more than a shrug and raised eyebrows, my eyes darting away coyly and playfully.

Inside he led me to the counter where a blonde waitress as young—and, I noted, at least as attractive—as myself leaned over and asked what we'd like. I also noted, with some satisfaction, that like myself she was not overly endowed or especially curvaceous, but her face was very pretty, and I found that I actually felt perturbed by the inviting look and open smile she flashed to my new guide. Of course, I then remembered rule number one, and took relief in the fact that they could not possibly be lovers. But then that didn't help *my* situation any!

He looked to me, and I shook my head and told him to choose for me. He ordered scrambled eggs and bacon for the both of us, then asked if they were fresh or from a supermarket. She informed him that, although they had lost a few of their livestock recently, we could still look forward to enjoying food that until recently lived among us in the village. I didn't exactly like the sound of that, but Bill closed his eyes and smiled, as if he could smell it in front of him already. "Mmm," he responded, and turned to me and explained, "Ever since my transformation I've had a preference for food that's been recently killed, as opposed to lying around in supermarkets treated with preservatives and the like."

"Is there a supermarket around here?" I asked, planning to cook my own meals if allowed. But he informed me that there wasn't, but some of the trips the *Canis sapiens* make into human towns are for such food and supplies, for their pens are often raided by wild animals and occasionally by one of their own.

I collapsed into a nearby chair at a table-for-two, and put my head in my hand, leaning my elbow on the wood table in front of me.

"The new girl, huh?" I heard the blonde remark. And then I could sense Bill taking the seat opposite me. I opened my eyes, and then apologized for being rude. "All this is just getting to me, ya know? Tell me, was it like that at first for you and then got easier after a while? And how long until I'm as gung-ho about this as you?"

"I don't know if you'll *ever* accept it," he answered honestly, and seemed sorry for it. "I've seen some Dingoes go through here who never make the adjustment. They're no longer with us, of course. I sure hope you decide you wanna stick around for a while. I mean, that's all it really takes. If you want something, you set your mind to it and you'll get by."

"You've only been here six months and you've seen enough Dingoes come and go? How long do we generally last here? I mean, how long can I expect to survive before I'm 'put out of my misery'?"

"A Dingo's life isn't always a long and fruitful one," Bill said, his ever-present smile tugged at its sides by some sad recollection. "But there've been some who can recall as many as twenty moves. And others who don't make it past one. I've been a Dingo since they first moved here, wherever *here* is. And I plan on being one of the ones who sees twenty more moves."

"You don't know where you are?"

"No. The first few days were a bit of a jumble. I originally came from DC. I was poking around, investigating a story about a fraudulent land claim that was uncovered and brought to my attention by this project developer who was interested in the property. But what I found instead—boy, oh boy. Same thing happen to you, I guess."

"No. I was actually contacted by the Professor—Do you know him?" I asked, to which he nodded affirmatively, "—to take down information and report to the world about their race. He wanted to let everyone know that they exist as a first step toward integration into our society."

Bill looked at me oddly, as if what I said didn't make sense. I added, "Jack and the rest caught up with him and silenced him, though, preserving their secret by murdering him and biting me."

Still Bill looked at me like what I said couldn't possibly be true. Then he shook it off and said, "As with me, you couldn't be trusted to not keep your mouth shut."

"Exactly. If I shared their plight, then I'd have to support their decisions."

"And do you?" he asked.

I took only a second before confiding in him. "No. And I despise them for what they did, both to me and to the Professor. That dear old man."

"Old *dog*. You gotta use the right terminology around here. Otherwise you might insult someone."

"So tell me more about your story," I prodded.

"Oh yeah, right," he said, as if he had forgotten he was in the middle of something. "Their time on that property was finished, so they had to move. I was brought along, not knowing up from down for a while. I had been bitten after a full moon, so I didn't experience the change, but my body was still in the midst of altering to its new metabolism and such. You're probably experiencing some of that— No? Well, it's different for everyone; you'll feel it soon enough. And then by your first full moon..."

"Wait, you're getting ahead. How did they do it to you?" I wanted to know, though I could not tell why I was so concerned.

Here, Bill paused, apparently reluctant or even embarrassed about revealing the details. He looked into my eyes for a few moments, and then gave himself a slight nod, deciding that he wanted to confide in me. "I was seduced, brought into a room by an attractive woman—knowing nothing about this werewolf business—and then, well..." His cheeks reddened at this point. "I was bitten in the middle of it, not knowing what was happening to me. Men rushed in; I was bound, gagged, stuffed into a sack. And carried away to a vehicle that drove for hours before stopping here, where they resettled. I was then given the initiation speech about my new life among them. To be honest, I was fascinated by it all. But I don't think I really believed I would be here forever—with the pack, I mean, not this location. I'm sure they'll be leaving *here* soon. It's no good for them to stay in any one place too long. You get too complacent and used to things, and that only makes it harder to accept 'change,' which is a necessary aspect of their world. Anyway, you probably feel that way too, like this is only a temporary thing." My silence confirmed this. "Well, I hate to be the one to break it to ya, honey, but this is it; you're in for the long haul. But it doesn't have to be so bad. You *can* make the best of it."

I dumped my head into my hands again and heard—and smelled—our orders being plunked down onto our table. I wondered if my sense of smell had gotten keener, because I couldn't recall when a food's aroma hit me so forcefully. Of course, it could've only been because I was starving from having skipped too many meals. But at that moment, I fully believed my body had already taken on a new, canine attribute.

And when I ate, I tore into my food with such gusto that I surprised myself. Bill merely raised an eyebrow in appreciation of my appetite as he ate his breakfast with considerably more refinement. But then he wasn't as famished as I!

In between bites, he told me more about the community. "We are so used to the rat race of our old lives, the nine-to-five grind, the constant rushing around to make appointments or keep deadlines, or whatever such nonsense used to matter to us. Here we have none of that. Sure, we have our jobs, but there really is little else, except socializing and learning to live at one with nature. I think you'll grow to like it after a while." I must not have looked convinced, for he added: "Okay, so you can easily get bored out here, especially if you're the type who always has to be doing something. That's why many, like Cookie or Jezebel's girls, stay on at their jobs longer, pulling multiple shifts just to keep busy. But you and I won't have that opportunity."

"You're a teacher here too?" I asked around a mouthful of eggs.

"Yes, and we only work when the little tikes are up for it, which is in the early morning, after their night romps and before their indoor escapades and naps. So what I do with my time is interview — I mean, get to know — our fellow Dingoes in the community. Do you wanna hear about them? There's a lotta fascinating stuff there. Do you know that one of Jez's prostitutes actually *was* a prostitute before getting bitten? And according to her, her job's more enjoyable — or rather I should say tolerable — now. Says the best part is that no one here wants oral sex from her."

I stopped chewing, thinking that over, but perhaps he thought I was offended by this little tidbit — and perhaps my cheeks did redden a bit — for he instantly apologized and went to change the subject. But I wasn't about to let him drop it, now that the subject was brought up. "Bill, it just dawned on me. Male Dingoes aren't allowed to use the services of Jez's girls; that would break their golden rule."

"That's correct," he replied flatly, perhaps fearing where this was going.

"So does that mean that you — I mean, that *they*, um..."

"Abstain?" he finished for me. I nodded. He shook his head and picked his words carefully: "The... needs of a male Dingo are usually catered to by the one who converted him. Provided that it was a female that did it, and depending on the... needs of the Dingo. And sometimes other females in the community might get... curious, and experimental."

"And they like to do it in wolf form," I added, just to confirm what I've been told.

"The males supposedly prefer it that way; the females... might be a little more flexible on that. For the woman, you see, there is a lot more that she can do in human form than she can in wolf form..." I believe we both reddened after that comment. Bill made an obvious attempt at a segue onto a different topic. "Cookie over there, and her brother who's working back in the kitchen, used to run a diner back in the world."

I let him steer our discussion back on its original course, and then remarked on his choice of wording. "'Back in the world.' I like that. You've used that prison jargon before, too."

"Well, let's face it. We are prisoners, even dangerous potential killers if the moon's just right. Under maximum security. Have you met our guards?" I didn't know what he meant and gave him a confused look. He elaborated: "They have dogs on the outskirts of the entire grounds, just to keep us in check."

"Not wolves?" I wondered.

"No. Aside from their endangered status, true wolves are a little skittish around this folk. Oh, not if they're in canine form. But they get completely spooked if they witness them change into a human. And even in human form... but then again I guess that's no different from how they feel about humans themselves. It's just that, when these guys are in human form, the wolves don't show any kinship with them, which has always puzzled me because I would've thought that scent and not sight would have mattered more and made the true wolves bond with them anyway, no matter what they looked like." He let that sink in before adding conspiratorially, "Unless, of course, it's not true that they're related to wolves at all."

"What are you talking about?"

He looked around first before answering. "It may just be the reporter in me, but I never take anything they tell me about themselves as the Bible truth. After all, they admit that they don't themselves know how they sprung about. Perhaps they were once human before undergoing something that forever altered them and their offspring. Coulda been some freak natural development, genetic evolution, scientific experiment... Hell, I wouldn't even rule out the supernatural or outer space. All I know is: wolves don't like 'em very much."

In the silence that followed I noticed that my plate was empty. He looked down and offered to call over Cookie for more. "She's really a wonderful girl," he explained. "It would be no trouble at all to her. Real name's Wendy Summers, she came fr—"

"Dogs," I interrupted, thinking I found a hole in his theory. "Dogs seem to love them though."

"They are 'man's best friend' after all," he responded matter-of-factly. "They're used to humans, have lived in their homes for thousands of years, have been fed and protected by them—"

"Okay, I get the picture," I conceded. "Maybe you have something there."

"Probably not," he suddenly said, changing gears unexpectedly. "I'm just an ex-reporter with too much time on his hands, playing devil's advocate." He paused, looking off into the distance, then turned to me and gave me a wide grin, to which I couldn't help but respond with the same. "Like take for instance this full moon business. Why only then?" he went on. "If they can change anytime they want, why does it only happen to us at night when the moon is full? If you ask me, I think that aspect of it stems from the human psyche, and has nothing to do with what we've become. Our kind has always been touched by the full moon in odd ways, sometimes extremely violent ways. Just ask any police officer and they'll tell you about the rise in violent crimes during that time. And of course there's the term 'lunatic' coming from the moon's name *Luna*."

I thought of offering my own experience, and that of many women, with bodily functions that coincided with the moon's cycle, but then I decided that talk of a sexual nature had already embarrassed both of us enough today—and we had only just met today!

"Boy, you sure do have a lot of time on your hands," I lamely said instead.

"Well, then there's my book."

"What?" This slipped out of my mouth rather quickly, no doubt betraying my sudden anxiety.

"I've been composing a book detailing life in the pack. Or at least my experiences with it."

There it was. My current life's ambition. My purpose, my goal, my destiny; the only thing I had left to give me hope. And he had beaten me to it. My tell-all expose on my treatment by this people, the thing that I had hoped would catapult me to the rank of true professional. No matter whether I wrote it or not, here was an experienced professional providing competition that I was not up to the task to counter. My insecurity was showing, but I hoped that he could not tell what had perturbed me; I'd rather keep my inferiority complex a secret.

"It'll never get published, of course," he continued, apparently without even noticing any change in my expression. "But it gives me something to do. And I am a writer, after all. Have to keep it up somehow, even if it is just for exercise. Maybe it'll be read by the pups someday, used in the classrooms to give them an idea of what we go through. Perhaps I'll go down in their history as another Susan B. Anthony or Martin Luther King, as inspiration for a movement towards betterment of the treatment of Dingoes."

He was smiling, but I wasn't sure he wasn't being serious.

"Would you like to read what I have so far?" he offered. "From one writer to another, I'd appreciate any criticism, or points that I haven't considered." I hesitated. "It'd be my honor," he concluded, "and you could get the dirt on all the other Dingoes and how they came to be here. It's real interesting to find out just what led them to decide what role to play in their new life here."

"Actually, on that score," I began, finding a way out, "I really think I should find out for myself. Ya know, do some interviewing of my own; keep the practice up as you were saying." If I did decide to go through with writing my accounts, the last thing I needed was another author claiming that I stole this or that from him. And whereas he had given up hope of leaving here and having it published, that was exactly the plan I had in mind.

He had finished his own meal, which took him longer due to his verbosity, so he gathered up our refuse and asked where he could take me next. I had already made up my mind. I wanted to get accustomed to my new home.

He walked me back, and I tried to keep track of our path so I could find my way back with ease; I was sure that the Social Center was one place I would want to be able to find so I could go there often. There's plenty to be learned here, and I felt that this was the place where I might get most of my dirt. And, of course, I'd have to know where to go for food.

At the door to my lodge, Bill pointed out his cabin across the way, asking me not to hesitate should I need him for anything. He assured me that, even though he doesn't spend much time there during the day, there was always someone around who could inform me of his whereabouts.

I thanked him and took his outstretched hand warmly to shake it. I observed that, as with the Professor, I genuinely liked and formed immediate trust in this man, and I was firmly convinced that if our circumstances were other than what they were I would have asked him inside, and been open to whatever he wanted to do once there.

Inside, alone, I found my personal effects, and sure enough my journal was among them. I read the foolish words I had written in it seemingly oh so long ago, and debated whether I should continue it or not. Those first few paragraphs were enough to make me laugh; how innocent and naïve I was, how unsuspecting. I wouldn't even acknowledge the possibility of sexual assault, and what actually happened was so much worse and life-altering. I had been writing down a few lines at a time, right up until I entered my bug and began my adventure. There was so much hope there, so much eagerness to make a name for myself. I considered starting over, but felt that that would not be true to my tale, so I continued from where I left off and wrote for the rest of the day until my stomach growled again. I planned on writing like this a little each day, recording any events of significance that I either experienced firsthand or witnessed through others.

As I prepared to set down my pen for the day, intent on seeking Bill out to have dinner with, I thought of the last words we had said to each other earlier and how they affected me emotionally. It took place after our parting handshake and his helpful offer to be of assistance.

"By the way," I had observed as he began to walk away, "you never mentioned who it was that seduced and bit you."

"The alpha's bitch, of course," he replied through tight lips.

Aryana. Will there be no end to the indignities this woman can inflict on others? No bottom to the depths of my hatred for her?

FIVE

I was not able to meet Bill after all last night, for when I opened the door Jack was there to introduce me to what would become my monthly ritual, and apparently Bill was already preparing for the same, if he wasn't already trussed up for the night. I must admit that I had forgotten all about this part of it at that moment, and so when I saw Jack standing there in the twilight with the length of chains in his hands I at first did not know what to think. I just reacted, startled, afraid, watching in frozen terror as he approached.

"Relax, there's no silver in it," he said reassuringly. "You might cut yourself while thrashing about in the night, and that would cause serious harm if we used such a lethal ingredient—probably even death." As I listened I was beginning to realize what they were for, and felt foolish for my overreaction. I backed up and let him enter, passing me by and heading straight for the empty corner of the room, beyond the bed. When I didn't follow, he motioned me to join him, again being anything but hostile about it. In fact, his demeanor could best be described as understanding, which I guess makes sense considering how many he's probably seen through this. They supposedly take their "responsibilities" seriously; I guess I would find out just how true this was.

When I got to where he knelt, I saw that the wood flooring in the corner had been broken away, and concrete had been poured into a hole that he assured me was deep enough for its task. A huge metal ring was embedded in the concrete, and it was through this that he began threading my chain. At the ends were open cuffs that were meant to ensnare my wrists, and I held my arms out to him, defeated and without hope, so that he could do what needed to be done. He placed the cuffs on the floor and rose, putting his hands into his pockets for God-knows-what new implement to present me with.

But when he withdrew his hands, they held only kerchiefs—thick, soft ones that he proceeded to tie around each of my wrists. He then bent down and lifted the cuffs, but they were held too close for him to reach me, and so I had to kneel down myself for him to put them on me, and with the cushioning he had provided I barely even felt the harsh metal bands.

"You don't have much room, because we don't want you to be able to reach anything and hurt yourself. As you can see, you can't even stand fully with them on. There's the wall behind you, of course, and the danger of you smashing your head against it, but it's just wood and in all likelihood you'll just claw at it in an attempt to get out. Any boards you break through can easily be replaced. Would you like me to stay until you fall asleep," he said, rising and looking down on me as though I were a new pet adjusting to my new home... and my new *leash*.

"No, I want to be alone," I responded, but not with the bitterness I had been feeling earlier. I was resigned and contemplative, wondering just how this full moon would affect me—and yes deathly afraid of it too. I sat with my legs crossed, staring at my bound wrists in silence. I did not even look up as he went to the front door.

"Oh, you were probably just about to get something to eat, weren't you? Well Cookie's obviously not there anymore either... I'll just bring you back a little something, okay? Then afterward you can use the bathroom and undress for the night." I heard the door close. And then heard it being fastened with a lock and chain on the other side.

Silence. I welcomed it and I feared it. The night held new meaning for me, and I would never again be able to look up at the moon without discomfort and dread. For even when it won't be full, it would just be a matter of days until... until I become a monster. I was afraid, and wished that Jack were here again. I would never admit it to him, but I actually wanted him to stay the night, to watch over me while I was not myself. But that could never happen anyway; his presence would probably make my inner demon react more violently. And also there was that special visit from the Hyena tonight, which I had wanted to witness. Why did he have to come on a full moon?

Jack did not take long to return, a fact I was grateful for though I tried not to show it. He released me from my chain and gave me a simple dish of some kind of oatmeal or other gruel, and some wine. He then instructed me to use the bathroom facilities for the night — run water if I had to in order to relieve myself now — and remove my clothing. When I told him that I had nothing to change into, he informed me that I would be sleeping nude, as all Dingoes do, otherwise the amount of clothing that would be torn through and shredded in the course of the monthly transformations would be outrageous.

"Nudity is our natural state," he remarked, taking a thick wool blanket from a dresser drawer and laying it out on the floor near the metal ring. "We think nothing of the sight of an unclothed human; in fact, that seems more correct to us."

"Plus there's the assertion that you don't find the human body to be at all attractive, right?" I added to see what his response would be. He simply stood there and waited, and so to test him I removed my clothing and handed them to him, impressed with the fact that he kept eye contact with me the whole time and didn't stare at my body as I undressed. "Nothing?" I prompted, nearly posing for some show of approval. I just couldn't believe that he didn't find anything worth looking at.

He glanced down at my body in a casual manner, not really lingering or looking too long at anything in particular until he stopped at my crotch. To that he commented: "Interesting pattern. Though like the rest of the girls I expect you'll quit shaving it at all, preferring, like the rest of us, to revel in your body hair."

I glanced down and was mortified to see a fragile white string clinging to my inner thigh. I reddened and went for my personal effects, praying and thanking God that I still had a few tampons left. I would be needing more soon, though, and hoped that someone would be able to loan me some or inform me where to get new ones when I run out. I retreated to the restroom and didn't come out until I was ready to face Jack again without shame. When I emerged he was sitting patiently waiting for me, and rose to get me set up once again with my cuffs and the kerchiefs and the chain. He did all this quietly, and still without any obvious glance toward my private parts, and then he went to the door. Before leaving he said, in a sympathetic tone that I was again not expecting from him, "Don't worry. I don't think it'll happen tonight. I think you'll be in the clear until the next full moon."

"There's always tomorrow," I said dispiritedly.

"No," he said emphatically. "The moon won't be full by then. Even if it's mostly full with just the trace of a shadow on its side, you're not going to change. I know it's bizarre, but that's the way it is, and we've got centuries of experience to know what we're talking about, so you can trust me on that."

"Crazy human psyche," I muttered.

"Nonsense. I know that's what your friend Bill believes, but he couldn't be further from the truth." How did he know about Bill? "The moon's attraction on everything on this planet is an actual, tangible thing, which for some reason your species can't even recognize or acknowledge. Just look at the beach, those waves pounding against the sand. Immense masses of water dragged around solely by the power of the moon, and your kind still thinks of it as some faraway thing which has no effect on our lives. Well let me tell you, a full moon, crisp and sharp, with no blurred or shaded edges, exerts a force so strong that it'd make ya believe in magic. I can't put into words... If only you could... Well, during the *day* when it's a full moon, maybe you'll be able to attune yourself to its pull and get a sense of what I'm talking about."

He was speaking quite passionately, obviously wanting me to understand the sensation he was having trouble describing. Somewhat frustrated in his attempt, he reluctantly gave up and turned to the door.

Then something dawned on me that I should have remembered before, and since he was in such a helpful and talkative mood I decided to take advantage of it and asked, "So which one was drugged, the meal or the wine?"

"The meal. I wouldn't dream of tainting such a fine beverage." With that said he left, and I was once again alone with my thoughts.

I tried to think of something that might brighten my mood, and found myself thinking of Bill, and wondering what he looked like lying naked in his room. I wanted to know the position he slept in, so I could accurately picture how his exposed penis lay. Was he on his side, with it resting softly against his inner thigh? On his back? But then it might drift to whatever side it had a tendency to lean. Or droop down between his legs. Or stand upright, in an effort to attain the moon. If he lay on his belly, would it right now be crushed under him against a hard wood floor? Wouldn't it be safer pressed against another body, a warm and welcome body, whose flesh was soft and yielding, as was intended for receiving such a firm appendage? Oh my God, I was getting myself hot! I was chained to a floor with my wrists ensnared by metal cuffs, and there I was fantasizing to the point of arousal!

Perhaps arousal would be the worst thing for me. Perhaps any form of excitement would make the transformation more severe, the experience more intense. Besides, love between Dingoes was forbidden. I had best put it out of my mind and think of something else, something that wouldn't excite me. I tried thinking of Jack, but realized that he brought forth an excitement of a different kind, a dislike as passionate as anything else could be. But he was gentle and considerate with me this night, and all I had to do was look down at my semi-protected wrists for evidence of this.

"If you're interested, I'd be willing to try it your way." Jack's offer suddenly came back to haunt me. No thanks! But again, the only way I would consent to do it with anyone else in wolf form would be if I were one myself, which would be impossible because I wouldn't be able to control myself in that form. I'd be a homicidal, cannibalistic beast, unable to reason with, much less be intimate with. Oh, if only I could be that way with Bill! Then at least we would both be the same type of creature; we both would have come from the same race.

And what would it be like to make love as such animals? I began picturing what our pairing would be like, providing that we were both rational and controlled during the encounter. And what if we changed all the way, instead of that *manimal* stage in between? Two complete wolves coupling in the night under the moon and the stars and nature herself. His fur warming the fur on my back; his arms locked on either side of me, pinning me in place; his legs bunched up behind my own to provide the power behind his rapid thrusts; his erect member...

Oh God, stop! My head was swimming. But I think it was the drug taking effect. But whether my sudden nausea was caused by this as well, or by the images I was conjuring up, I could not be certain. I slumped down against the flooring, my head crashing none too gently against the unyielding wood surface, and my eyes were beyond my ability to keep open. I was asleep.

• • • • •

At some point in the night I groggily awoke to the sound of laughter and barking, but amidst this was a tortured howling that I wondered if I myself were making. I knew the other sounds were coming from the little celebration they were having outside, but a glance down at my still-human form convinced me that the howling was coming from someone else, and from someplace quite near at that. I drew the wool blanket over me from where it remained folded by the ring, and then I was under again, held by the effects of the sleeping draught that I had imbibed in that bland, tasteless gruel. When morning came, I had to be given a potion to counter the original one—that's how strong it was. I looked up to see that it was Aryana who had given me the antidote. As my head cleared I heard her tell me that I shouldn't be late my first day of work. Then she was gone, and so too were the cuffs and chain, replaced by a simple dress almost identical to the one I wore the day before, and I was left alone to dress and prepare for my first day as an active member of their community. *My* community. What a night.

But as strange and uncomfortable as my night was, the following day would top it in spades. Bill was already up and gone, and I got lost looking for the building that acted as their school. Remember, all the cabins looked the same, and I had only been shown the way once, and to be honest I had a lot swimming around in my head the previous day to be that observant. I had still been trying to swallow all that happened to me and coming to terms with my new situation to pay too much attention to the lay of the land. I did make it to the Social Center, the one place I had made sure I knew how to get to, and was about to go in to ask Cookie for directions when I was accosted by a male in his fifties, an "old dog" by their standards.

"Ah, you must be the new girl—the journalist—that I heard about," he said to me with an almost intoxicated tone. I didn't smell alcohol on his breath, which would have been easy to detect since he was leaning in and invading my personal space quite a bit, but he was definitely soaring from the effects of something. "I had hoped to meet you before I left. Looks like my luck's holding out."

"You're the Hyena," I realized, to which he nodded his head with wild, uncoordinated swings.

"Maybe at Jezebel's later?" he suggested, his eyes and mouth open wide, his tongue toying with his teeth in an overtly suggestive manner. "I'm looking forward to seeing you there," he added, closing his mouth but widening his eyes further and tilting his forehead in my direction as if awaiting a response.

Oh, I had a response for him, but I bit back the "In your dreams" I had wanted to say and settled for a harmless and noncommittal "I bet you are."

He smiled idiotically and headed in a direction that would probably take him straight to the pleasure house in question. I had so wanted to meet him the day before, thinking him to be a wise and interesting personality, one whom I could learn plenty of bizarre facts and stories from, but apparently all he could teach me was how to party. I was glad that I was not able to attend his big event last night and grateful that his visit fell on a full moon.

Wendy Summers—Cookie—suddenly appeared at the establishment's entrance. She handed me a baggie with some fruit and cold vegetables in it, apple slices and cut carrot sticks mostly, and told me to hurry to get to my job, pointing out the way and providing landmarks I hadn't noticed the day before. I kissed her cheek in grateful thanks and proceeded on my way, happy to report that I made it the rest of the way without incident, but I still was a little late. Bill Jensen was waiting for me outside, stating the obvious. "You're late. Let me help you get set up with Jez and the class, okay? How are your wrists?" he asked as we walked into the lodge.

I looked down at them confused, and then realized he was referring to my wearing cuffs for the first time. "Healed up nicely," he observed.

"Oh, no, I didn't change last night. And Jack wrapped my wrists up nicely with scarves so I wouldn't feel anything. And I practically didn't."

Bill's face looked confused about that, and I suppose it was a pretty odd courtesy to extend to someone with healing powers. But then I probably didn't have that yet either.

"Anyway," he said, shrugging that aside and moving on to a new topic. "I'm sorry if I ruined your sleep last night."

Now it was my turn to look confused.

"I hear that I was howling so much I was practically spoiling the celebration."

"That was you?" I asked. "I did wake up briefly to the sounds of it, but then their drug took me under again. You sounded tortured." I added sympathetically.

"Who knows. I mean, I don't know what I'm like normally when I've transformed, but according to those familiar with me I've been more agitated than usual this month. It was even suggested that it's because I'm zoning in on someone who's currently in heat—" He broke off, embarrassed and unable to go on. "Uh," he stammered, looking around, "there's the principal's office—Jezebel, you know her. You'll have to see her first. Then I'll walk you to your class, which is in the adjoining cabin.

I left him without a comment on what we were previously discussing and saw beyond Jez's office that the back of the lodge led to a brief outdoor section that connected to two more lodges behind it. I had been wondering how they could fit more than a few classes into one lodge, and now it became apparent. They could probably run up to as many as six classes at a time here, and more if those back lodges connected to further ones beyond. In I stepped to find Principal Jezebel, the Madam from the cathouse, dressed not much differently than when I saw her last at that other location, except with perhaps an additional layer of clothing.

She didn't ream me out, and I wondered why everyone seemed so intent that I not be late—as if Jez would beat me or fire me for such an indiscretion—and after her perfunctory orientation speech I decided to ask Bill about it as he led me out the door to one of the back lodges, where both of our classes were.

"Oh, that. It's just that the pups will only stay so long for education. After a long night, they're not too eager to have to sit through our lecturing and just want to go to bed. So, the earlier you start teaching, the sooner they can get on to their sleep and to the other things that they value in life. The adults take seriously the pups' education, even if the pups themselves don't. Just like with humans," he concluded brightly.

"Here we are," he said, as we stood before a door that was more ominous to me than any I had approached in my life. I would be terrified facing a group of human kids, but this group would be even more intimidating to me. And I didn't even have a syllabus to work from. Jez said that I would find one in my desk, but that for my first day I should just introduce myself and get to know the kids, telling them about my life and the world I came from, and seeing if they would open up to me about themselves.

"And here I go," I said with a weak smile, opening the door, entering my classroom, and closing the door behind me. I opened my mouth to introduce myself and tell them my name, but instead I screamed as loud as I could. Bill rushed in and I clung to him, burying my head in his shoulder as he asked, "What happened?"

I felt foolish. But really, weren't they all supposed to be in human form? How else could we speak and interact? I wasn't prepared to see a roomful of wolves all watching me, seemingly snarling (was that their attempt at a smile?), and so I lost my head and played right into their little prank.

"Oh, very funny," Bill was saying to them sternly. "Now you all stop that and make yourself presentable for your new teacher, come on." When I dared to raise my head, blushing from the humiliation, I saw that almost all of them were now human-looking young boys and girls, and that they fortunately had clothes with them to wear. "The ones in the back are too young and cannot change form yet. But they like them to sit in and learn behavior from the older ones, and you might catch them trying to change their limbs or their face—it's freaky at first, I know. You'll do all right; trust me. And now I've gotta get to my own group of little darlings." And with that he took me by the shoulders and set me upright to face my class, and left.

As I was to learn, there were only three classes including my own, and each had about eight to ten pups in it. I had eight, but only six of them were old enough to participate, leaving the two young ones that were still in wolf form. And that was not counting one Dingo (there was one in each class), who they had apparently locked in the closet in order to pull off their joke on me. They now let him out, and he took a seat without looking at me. I think he was ashamed to have been part of it, even if forced, and so he could not face me just yet.

The ages ranged from the little two-year-olds in the back to a scrappy male of thirteen; there were three girls and five boys, two of whom were the young pups, and the Dingo was a seven-year-old boy. My heart instantly went out to him.

"My name is Miss Journal, but you can call me Beverly," I began, but the oldest boy wouldn't leave it at that.

"Isn't your name *ow-ow-owoo* or something undecided yet?" he taunted. I had a heckler in my class.

"Well then *you* can just call me Miss Journal, okay?" I shot back at him. I then began to tell a little about myself, trying hard not to play favorites but constantly catching myself addressing the young Dingo more than the rest. As I mentioned bits of my life and career, my young jokester spoke up again.

"Oh come on," he said. "You know what we really want to hear about?"

"And what's that?" I replied a bit testily.

"*You know,*" he said leeringly, and I must admit that I was already growing tired of his humor.

"No I don't," I said. "Why don't you come up here and try to explain what it is you're trying to say." I hoped that this would embarrass him, but he obviously enjoyed such attention. He swaggered up to the front of the class, right next to me, with a grin that stretched from ear to ear. I took a seat at my desk, not wishing to share the stage with him for whatever he had planned. I wasn't sure if their aging was much different than our own at this young age, but just like any thirteen-year-old human boy, there seemed to be only one thing on his mind.

"What we'd—" he began, but I interrupted him just to throw him off his stride.

"Please state your name before you ask your question."

"My human name is Mack, but everyone calls me Mackey," he said after faltering slightly, and then resumed his cockiness. "And what we'd like to know," he said, dragging out the last word and facing me at the side of my desk, "is if you've tried one of these yet and if you liked it more than what you're used to."

I followed his eyes to his crotch—no surprise there—but instead of just the erection I had already assumed he was sporting, there was a strange motion from inside his pants. The bulge pressed agonizingly against the front of his jeans, it surged upward and outward to unbelievable proportions, and then it pulsed and throbbed with the intensity and fury of a fist trying to push its way through, the denim material straining under the stress it was not designed to endure. It squirmed and wriggled like a snake, and did more tricks the likes of which no human could ever achieve. This opened up new possibilities to me of the nature of shape-shifting, and I gasped and blushed—as was his intention—at the ideas that dawned upon my feral imagination.

He was smiling wickedly and the class was snickering mercilessly—with one obvious exception—and I was about to tell him to sit down but I had not found my voice yet. This made me even more embarrassed and angry, and I was about to yell when a better idea hit me. I cleared my throat so that the words could come out clear, and then said to him playfully, "Why, Mackey, I didn't know you were a Coyote."

I wasn't sure if the effect of using the slang expression would be what I was hoping for, but as I saw the blood drain from his face and heard the uproar of laughter from the other children who chimed in with sing-song taunts of *"Mackey's a Coyote,"* I knew that my words had struck home. I was never more pleased with myself than just then. I knew that he was just a child with raging hormones, but he would one day be an adult male, and as I looked him in the eye as his expression changed to one of mortification, I felt as if I had delivered a blow against every lecherous boss or poor-intentioned suitor that I and the rest of my sisterhood had to live with and endure on a daily basis. I was sure I would be ashamed of these feelings one day, but at the moment I reveled in my success.

The kids were still chanting their taunt at him when I felt he had had enough and that I should restore order to the class. "Please take your seat, Mister Mack; we have a lot more to cover this morning." We actually didn't, as this first class was mostly introductory for all of us, but it gave him an excuse to sit down and a reason for the children to be quiet. The rest of the class was without incident, except that I couldn't help sensing a note of despair in the Dingo boy's forlorn expression. His name was Richard Hasselhoff, and he was "Ricky" to everyone. He wasn't being shunned by the rest of the kids, and I suspected that the presence of Dingoes was quite common and accepted by the children, as it was by the adults, but after the treatment I had experienced so far I would assume that all Dingoes were considered nothing more than second-class citizens in this society, and certainly expendable ones at that, should an emergency evacuation be in order.

When class was over, Bill was there at the door to my room, and after all my students had filed out he came in and sat in one of the seats in the front. "How was it?" he asked, and I sighed and wearily gave him a brief rundown of the events that transpired since he had last seen me after my earlier indignity at the beginning of class. He chuckled when appropriate, expressed concern where required, and was the perfect audience for my tale. "Aren't you glad it was only for three hours?" he asked when I was done.

"Three hours?" I said in disbelief. "I could've sworn it was twice that."

"But still, aren't you glad you chose this profession? In Jez's other establishment you'd still be on call for the rest of the day. Plus there's the little matter of having to cater to all those wolfmen out there. . . Or, after what you've seen today, is that a more intriguing notion?"

I looked at him dryly. "I should never have told you about that," I replied. He laughed.

"This was just your initiation; tomorrow won't be so bad."

"I've had enough initiations. Now I just want to go to bed." I was looking him in the eye when I said this, and hoped it didn't look like an invitation. If he registered the slightest discomfort or embarrassment, it was gone before I could confirm it, and he proceeded to escort me out of the building to walk me back. We talked more as we went.

For small talk, Bill provided some interesting observations, such as how *Canis sapiens* are predominantly left-handed the way humans are more commonly right-handed. "You didn't notice that Jack is a lefty?"

"No," I had to admit, "but then I never really saw him write or eat or do anything where it would be noticeable." Well there was him chaining me up for the night, but I did have a lot on my mind at the time. And I was drugged too. Anyway, I neglected to mention it.

"And notice how all the males choose simple, common, everyday names for what we should call them in our human tongue, whereas the females show a preference for exotic-sounding ones. Leilani, Aryana, Jezebel, and Fiona."

This I might have registered on a subconscious level. I *had* thought that Aryana and Jezebel had unusual names when I first heard them. And I had a Leilani and a Fiona in my class. I recalled something Aryana had said to me and asked him, "Can you smell the difference between us? Between humans and them, I mean."

"Hah, no. They like to act like there's some obvious distinction and that nasally we're the equivalent to being blind or deaf—which I suppose we are. But no, I don't know any Dingo who's ever been able to *smell* a difference. *I* can tell a difference from other things, the way they walk for instance. Their whole bearing is different from ours; there's a confidence and an animal character to them which I think makes them stand out like a sore thumb. But otherwise their impersonation of us is... perfect."

After a moment's silence, he provided another tidbit that wasn't as pleasing to learn. "Be choosy about what bathrooms you use; most are sadly neglected and in disgusting shape." I furrowed my brow and was about to inquire why, but he already began explaining. "They don't use bathrooms; they go out in the woods, usually in wolf form, so they don't ever have any reason to go into one. But the ones in the more public spots like the Social Center, which are commonly visited by Dingoes, are better attended to, usually by the Dingoes ourselves." He shook his head. "Ya know, we get all the worst of it and none of the perks. I'd love to know what it's like to run and romp under the moon on all fours, to shape-shift—under *my* control, not unconsciously and viciously. Then we have to watch out with silver. And chocolate."

"'Scuse me," I interrupted, stopping him with a hand to his chest.

"Oh yeah, you know how chocolate is poisonous to dogs. Well, same goes for wolves, now doesn't it?"

I may be exaggerating but I believe my head began reeling. There were a lot of adjustments that I might be able to live with over time, but not this. "No chocolate," I breathed, "ever?"

He treated it with the level of seriousness I felt it demanded. With his hands on my shoulders, he mournfully informed me, "I'm sorry to be the one to break this to you. But it's true. You can't touch another chocolate candy again ever. Artificially flavored chocolate items are all right, but not the real thing. See what I mean? All the bad stuff..."

"And none of the perks," I finished for him. "I didn't sign up for this," I joked weakly.

"Wrong metaphor," he instructed. "That's the military. My prison motif is more apt."

"It sure is," I agreed. Although I still prefer to think of it as them having murdered me instead of just locking me up. "The Hershey Kiss!"

"Nope. Can't have them anymore either, I'm afraid."

"No, no. I have a Hershey's Kiss in my bag. Old, perhaps six months old, and probably hard as a rock..."

"Well I hope you're not planning on eating it. Even though I know many dogs who've scarfed down huge quantities of chocolate at their owners' holiday parties and didn't even get sick enough to throw up, much less die from it, I wouldn't take any chances. We're not exactly like dogs. Look how silver acts in our bloodstream. I've never seen but I've heard of how one of us can suffer and die from it; it isn't pleasant."

"It's kinda like a suicide pill prisoners of war take when they can't take it anymore in captivity, huh?" I said, finding my comparison to be rather clever. He just looked at me gravely.

"I know you're having a hard time with your adjustment. But it's all pretty new for you still. I'd feel a helluva lot better if you'd give it to me."

"No way, *Kimo sabe*," I responded teasingly. "And give up my only lifeline..." I was about to clutch my bag tightly to my side when I suddenly realized that I didn't have it on me. "My bag!" I exclaimed. "I must have left it back in my classroom."

We backtracked to the school, and as I was about to follow Bill inside I observed a few of the children playing by that small pen I had noticed the other day. This time, however, it was not empty; little Ricky Hasselhoff was penned inside as if he were an animal, to the amusement of the rest of the children, who pointed and laughed and called him "little Dingo dog."

"What is going on here?" I screamed, making the children jump and turn around in surprise. "Who put him in there?" I demanded to know, adding a stern "Answer me" when none of them spoke up.

The youngsters shuffled and looked down, until their eyes eventually sought out one of the boys, who remained stock still and silent. It wasn't that troublesome Mack; he wasn't even here. These were mostly the younger kids from the classes, under ten years old. To their credit they didn't turn into wolves and snarl at me until I fled screaming—which I would have done! No, they hung their heads with guilt just like ordinary human children.

"Open that thing and let him outta there," I said, addressing the one they had unwittingly singled out, a boy named Paul who was seemingly the same age as Ricky. He did so without delay, and I took Ricky by the hand and began leading him from the group. He was filthy from the mud in the caged area, but little boys don't ever mind being dirty, so I knew that his downtrodden expression could only have come from their debasing treatment of him. "Would you like to come with me?" I asked him gently, to which he nodded slowly, without meeting my eyes.

The boy responsible for his incarceration spoke up, with a trace of uncertain anxiety to his tone: "But he's my responsibility. I made him."

"And look at the job you've done of it," I snapped back. "Would you treat a pet like this?"

"Well he kinda is a..." he began, but instantly shut up when I glared at him furiously.

Suddenly Bill, who I hadn't even noticed throughout the whole incident, emerged from the school building carrying my bag. He handed it to me and tentatively asked, "Everything under control here?"

"Nothing I can't handle," I replied, then shooed the children away, saying, "Isn't it time for you to be in bed or curled up on a mat or something?" We walked back toward my cabin again, with Ricky between us, holding our hands. "So did you extract my suicide pill?" I asked Bill. "That *is* why you went in ahead of me, isn't it? I might have needed your help out there. Did you think of that?"

"Not from them. I know those kids; they won't give you any trouble. Jez wouldn't saddle you with any difficult pups, you being new and all."

"Oh, but she gave me Mackey, didn't she? And don't try to switch the subject. Did you take it?"

"No, I... didn't want to leave you out there by yourself too long just in case you needed another adult for moral support and such. So I hurried right out. And don't fret Mackey. He's at that age..."

"Yeah, I know people I've dated and worked for who still never recovered from being 'that age.'"

"Well, I think they wanted you to know him because of what he might become. The next alpha. Jack's sorta groomin' him for the position."

"Is he Jack's son?" I asked, suddenly fearful of how much — or rather how *little* — authority I would be allowed to exert over the boy.

"I'm sure he'd like to think so. But I seriously doubt if even he knows."

"What?" I was genuinely surprised at this. "But I thought wolves mated for life, or some such nonsense. And isn't Aryana the alpha's bitch? What does she have to say about that? She's not exactly the type to roll over and ignore it."

"To be honest, I don't think they know much at all about what real wolves do. The only thing about them that resembles wolf life is when they're in wolf form running around under the stars. Otherwise, they've spent so much time trying to be like us, they've lost touch with their cultural identity. As for mating, they're more like us. They'll tell you how in a real wolf pack only the alpha is allowed to mate, and how they're more progressive than that."

"Only the alpha," I marveled, and instantly recognized the impossibility of trying to enforce that among this bunch. "Is that true?"

"Who knows. Most of them have never even seen a normal wolf, endangered as they are and all that. Plus, as I mentioned, regular wolves aren't too crazy about being around them. I know this because one Hyena actually brought a couple with him on leashes as a special treat, sort of like show-and-tell. I saw him arrive with them and how they acted. He got so far as to introduce them to some pups in their natural form. And that went fine until they started turning human. First chance they got, they took off and evaded all the trackers that were sent out after them.

"So anyway, in their 'progressive' society, which is more involved and complex than your ordinary wolf pack's, anyone is allowed to mate, and most of them form couples and families just like you or me, but the alpha, and *only* the alpha, is allowed to mate with all the females in his pack. This is because they want to pass on all the alpha's strong leadership traits as best as they can, and the more partners he tries it with, the higher the chances of a successful pregnancy by him." I thought about the rationale behind that, and saw some sense to it in a weird, alien kinda way. But I wasn't as impressed as Bill was, and he went on to extol the position. "We're not talking about a presidency; I mean, who would let their president sleep with their wife? A regency is closer, but more like the usurpers of old, barbaric times. An alpha must instill complete confidence and have the love and support of his pack; otherwise he'll be challenged by someone out to prove he can do more for the pack. They would give their alpha anything, and if someone doesn't prove himself worthy of the title, his replacement is sure to assert himself and strip him of his rank. Forget votes; forget democracy; socialism and communism come to mind, but here they work as intended, to the betterment of the community or the pack."

Whew. Ever hear about those topics you should never bring up in conversation with someone new? I believe religion is high on the list, but politics is one that, as far as I'm concerned, should come in first place every time. Too many shades of gray involved, as well as too many uninformed opinions. Now I'm not saying Bill doesn't know what he's talking about, but listening to him speak passionately about a society he wasn't even born into did not fill me with the awe he no doubt intended to instill in me. My feelings remained unchanged, and quite honestly, at the time all I cared about was looking after poor Ricky.

"And how was your night, sweetie?" I asked him.

He looked up at me and smiled sadly, and I remarked to myself how a child of his age should not even know how to smile in a sad way, only with joy. "I slept fine last night, and the night before that, but the night before that wasn't much fun at all," he said softly.

"How many nights do you have to put up with this?" I said, turning to Bill. "I thought there was only one full moon a month."

"Yes, *technically* there is," he replied, "but twenty-four hours before and after what scientists would acknowledge as a full moon, it looks every bit as full to the naked eye. Even longer, except that on careful observance you can make out a trace of a shadow, and subconsciously we can tell. Plus, with our twenty-twenty vision, we all see the moon in roughly the same way."

I thought about this, but suddenly Bill was off again on another one of his impassioned speeches. "Don't you see? This only goes to prove what I said about this all being psychological. He probably told you that only during a full moon can we feel its power and effect over us. But what he doesn't know—and I'm not about to be the one to debate him on this—is that the phase of the moon has nothing to do with its gravitational effect on Earth. Tides are stronger when the moon is closer in its orbit to us, and has nothing to do with how much sunlight it reflects back at us! If they want to come up with a way to cure us of this curse, the answer lies in *psych*ology, not *bio*logy."

"Well, here's my new home," I said, unnecessarily perhaps but enough to give the hint that our conversation on this topic should end. It wasn't that I had no interest in what he was saying, or that my attraction to him had in any way dwindled; it was just that at that moment I had a new concern that was occupying my thoughts, that poor, sweet little boy, Ricky Hasselhoff. I asked the child if he would like to come inside and stay with me for a bit, to talk if he wanted, or just to have a place to sit if he didn't want to speak. He nodded and I led him inside. At the door I turned and gave Bill a kiss on the cheek, thanking him for his help back at class. He then left me alone with my new friend, and I closed the door on his retreating form, hoping that this child would be just what I needed to take my mind off other things. And cold showers never worked for me anyway!

SIX

I looked up at the dark shadow that is the moon in its new moon phase and wondered why that damn satellite must do this to us, make monsters of angels. Yes, that's right, I said "new moon." It has been two weeks since I wrote last, a busy two weeks. At first my time was occupied in a pleasantly diverting way, but then things changed, and grew dark—dark as that cowardly guilty moon that is now hiding from me—and I had not the heart to put pen to paper to recount what had happened. And so that's why I waited to write this important chapter in my life, waited until I was able to do so without falling to pieces. And I must confess, this is proving to be more difficult than I thought.

Let me start with something easier to recall.

. . . . .

The day I took Ricky in was spent quietly, as I let him get accustomed to being around me without forcing conversation or prying questions upon him. It was a pleasant day, and I could almost forget my own troubles as I pondered on his. For whatever I was going through, I could only imagine how much more complicated it must be for him, a child, all alone and separated from his parents. I was bursting to have him tell me the story of how he was captured and changed, but I knew that this would only scare him away this early in our acquaintance. I had to be patient.

Aryana paid me a visit that day, noting the boy's presence and never taking her eyes off him, even as she informed me of the special event that would take place that night, a celebration for the sake of the Dingoes, who were unable to take part in the previous night's festivities.

I remarked that I didn't have a thing to wear — quite literally — pointing out that I would probably get along better with a wardrobe of my own, kept within my room. She agreed that I needed some clothing, and told me that she would return later with something fresh for me to wear for the evening, and then I could discuss with Jezebel that night what articles of clothing I could remove permanently from her brothel. I opened my mouth to suggest that I pick my own attire for the party, but she had already snapped on her heels and was out the door before I could speak.

I looked at Ricky, who seemed to be in the process of trying to make himself invisible — obviously deathly afraid of Aryana, and I couldn't blame the poor child — but now that she had gone he looked up at me and simply said, "She's mean."

"She is, at that," I replied with a sigh and a smile.

"I better go," he said. "It didn't look like she wanted me here."

"Ricky, you don't need her approval to visit me, and I don't need her permission to have you here."

"I know, but I still better go," he responded sadly.

I couldn't expect much more for our first day; it was actually an accomplishment that he came inside with me in the first place. "Well, all right," I said pleasantly, "but any time you want to drop by, even if it's just to say hello as you go somewhere else, you feel free to do so."

"Okay," he said as he sprinted for the door. He opened it and, his face half hidden by the door, he smiled and said, "Thanks." Success! I had reached him.

I collapsed on the bed and figured that I had better rest up if I were going to be out all night. But it was awfully hard to sleep when it was so early and so bright outside, so after trying unsuccessfully for ten minutes to will myself to sleep, I gave up and decided to go outside. After all, I had pulled all-nighters plenty of times before. It would just make me sleep all the more soundly the next morning. Except that I would first have to endure my second day of class with my little monsters, and I couldn't go to it exhausted or worse yet inebriated!

I went to the Social Center to see if Cookie had something that would make me sleep in the afternoon—not a potion like they gave me during the full moon, but something that normal people might take to get some rest. Perhaps wine would do the trick.

Sure enough, at the Social Center I found Bill, wolfing down Cookie's cooking like it was going to be his last meal ever. I told him to take it easy, as there was bound to be lots of good food at the celebration, especially since it was being held for us.

"You heard about it, then."

"Yes, good news travels fast," I said. "I was looking for something to knock me out so that I can stay up all night without being a zombie tomorrow in class. And I don't mean one of their special knockout drops either. Know of anything that'll do the trick?"

"Eat as hearty as I am now, and you'll be out the rest of the day," he suggested.

"Yeah, and I won't be able to fit into any of the clothes Jez gives me. How can you eat like that?"

"Enhanced senses," he replied. "The sense of smell aids in our tasting things, so with our new heightened senses, food tastes like nothing I've ever had before. Just wait'll yours kicks in. Eating will be an entirely new experience for you; you'll probably gain ten pounds the first month like the rest of us. And speaking of which, has anything changed yet for you?"

"Nope. I'm happily human in every way still," I lied, recalling that my feelings for a certain alpha bitch were more feral than human, but not wishing to share that. "But tell me, are there any other good things to look forward to when it does finally happen?"

"Actually, yes," he said after swallowing down a mouthful of grub. "But it probably doesn't affect you. You don't wear contacts, do you?"

"No, I've got 20/20 vision. Why?"

"Well, when I first arrived, I wore glasses..."

"Are you trying to tell me that—"

"My rejuvenating abilities cured what was wrong with my vision. My eyes healed themselves, as it were," he said, beaming with a pleasure the likes of which I could only imagine. I had plenty of friends who wore contacts, and for them the possibility of having their eyes suddenly... heal themselves was beyond the fathomable. It would be, for them, an actual miracle. I began to understand, if only slightly, the measure of delight that Bill obviously felt about his transformation. But for me, it didn't mean anything. No perks still; only the bad things.

"Is Cookie around?" I asked after looking around and not seeing her.

"No, she's busy with plans for tonight's event. She may be a Dingo, and the celebration may be for her as well as the rest of us, but she's also the catering crew. Besides, you wouldn't want our culinary details handled by one of *them*, do you?"

"No, you got a point. I just wish she had something to make me sleep in the middle of the day."

"Let's see. You could read the book I've been writing. That might do the trick. Or I could try and bore you to sleep by talking on and on."

I laughed. "I'd settle for some wine right about now. But you know what? Maybe a nice long walk will work. Checking out the grounds for as far as they'll let me tread."

"Want some company?" came his predictable offer, which I gently declined.

"No, you finish your private feast here. I've got to get familiar with the lay of the land anyway. So then I won't be late for work again."

This was true too, and he fortunately left it at that and continued stuffing his face. If he joined me and talked like he always does, I would be too distracted to familiarize myself with the directions and locations of things, and then I would feel like I had not progressed at all since my first day here.

I walked unhindered throughout the community, their spies obviously staying well out of sight, for I knew that I must have been under surveillance, especially along the outskirts of the cabins and lodges. There, just meters from the outlying woodland areas, I remained unaccosted, though I was sure that my observers were no doubt watching my every move from the trees. I traversed the entire grounds a second time to ensure that I knew my way around, and then turned sharply on my heels to return to my cabin, only to catch a wolf peering at me from beside a nearby lodge. That in itself was not surprising, as I had been convinced anyway that I was being followed, but what surprised me was the canine's reaction upon being sighted. He — I'm only assuming it was a "he" but it could just as easily have been a bitch — nervously looked away, and then subconsciously stepped in an unsure direction before trotting away out of sight. He was gray in color and on his head was an unusually patterned tuft of white fur. I could only imagine that perhaps he was an adolescent just undergoing training to be a guard but not having any experience yet at it, except that — my inability to determine age among them notwithstanding — this didn't seem to be a young wolf.

I didn't see him or any wolves other than the occasional townsfolk in human form the rest of the way back, and I reached my room without being approached by anyone. In fact, none of the *Canis sapiens* that I passed said hi, nodded an acknowledgment, or would even look me in the eye. I assumed that this was indicative of some class structure among the community, with Dingoes ranking somewhere below dirt, despite their assurances to the contrary.

I went inside and plopped down on my bed again, and this time I felt the comforting lull of tranquillity that usually precedes a restful nap. I sank into the sensation and dreamily closed my eyes and turned my head experimentally to each side, searching for that best angle and position that would put me into a relaxing dream state.

A walk in nature seemed to agree with me, and I fell into a sleep that boasted of romps of young lovers upon grassy knolls and a wonderful odor emanating from a carefully prepared picnic basket, carried along on a cool, wet breeze that suggested a nearby brook or stream. The lovers, not surprisingly, transformed into myself and Bill, and our lovemaking was every bit as delicious and "human" as I could have wished it to be. My naked back pressed the pliant blades of grass against the earth, and the cool dew, along with the winds caressing the blades against my exposed skin, caused a ticklish sensation that sent tremors coursing through my body, while the hot invasion of my inner flesh from above provided tremors of another kind. I gripped Bill's arms, his muscles locked in the effort of supporting his body over mine, and I wrapped my legs around his, intertwining our limbs in a way that disrupted his thrusts enough for me to savor the contact between our bodies. I writhed against the damp ground, repositioning my legs higher up so that he could resume his motions unimpeded. I tossed my head from side to side, catching a glimpse of someone watching us. I looked back to where the distant figure was, only now it was much closer, shaking its head "no." It was young Ricky, and inside I guiltily knew I should stop, but instead I closed my eyes and reveled in the spasms that rocked my body, exciting Bill enough to climax himself and spasm in time with my own.

Whew. I knew that it was not something that could ever be allowed to happen in real life, but that didn't mean that I couldn't dream about it. In fact, that might even help, act as a catharsis for what I wasn't getting while awake, satisfying urges that didn't look like they would ever be fulfilled. Yes, I knew that I was only kidding myself and that this would not have the desired effect that I just described. It would probably even have the opposite effect, and leave me in even more need for it. But what could I do? I couldn't control what I dreamed about.

The sounds of someone entering my room forced me groggily awake. From the bed where I lay I looked over at Aryana, who entered the room boldly at first, only to hesitate and sniff the air. After but a second, she looked down at me and said, "You're in a state of arousal. When was the last time you engaged in sexual activity?"

I should have been outraged by her inquisitiveness, but at that moment I was too amused by the clinical way she asked me. I did not, however, provide a response.

"A couple of days?... Weeks?... Don't tell me it's been months!"

"What does that have to do with anything?" I suddenly blurted out testily.

"Oh, nothing," she replied coyly. "It's going to be a real interesting night, what with you driving all the Dingoes mad this soon after a full moon." She sniffed in deeply. "Well, at least you're heat seems to have finished."

I thought about it and realized that she was right, that it *was* practically over.

"Looks like I made the right move by not bringing you any fresh underwear."

"What?" I leaped up, inspecting what she had brought me from Jez's place.

She handed me one single garment, a very brief dress that looked like it would cling unforgivingly to my every curve, or lack thereof. "You won't need a bra with this; it isn't meant to be worn with one," she instructed me. "As you can see, the fabric crosses over from one breast to the other, overlapping and at the same time crossing under each one so that they are held up and given plenty of support, which you soft humans seem to need so much of. As for panties, I thought you might like to try it our way: *without.* You might find that you enjoy it like that. It actually can be very freeing. You have those tampon things anyway, if you still think you might need it tonight, but otherwise I think you will feel more comfortable than you've ever been in your life. And more sexual, although I don't know how much we want to encourage that, with the male Dingoes still driven by the moon's effects. Oh, they won't be turning into wolves literally, but you might just have them gnashing their teeth and banging their heads against the walls. I sure can't wait until you stop having that every month."

"Huh—*you* can't," I muttered. Although actually I was glad I still had it, glad that I hadn't yet lost any of what made me different from them, even something as unpleasant as my period.

"Do you want help getting into it; I can show you just how to wear it for best effect?" she offered.

"No, I think I know my body well enough, and have been dressing to show it off long enough, that I can manage on my own, thanks."

"Well, just remember, at the feast there'll be a lot to sample, and you should keep your mind open and try all that there is to experience tonight."

I knew that she was talking about sex—sex with one of them!—and that she most likely knew how I felt about that, but I wasn't about to let her get my goat. "Yes, wearing this I just might not be able to keep Jack away," I taunted.

"Yes, he *was* the one who bit you, and so you *are* his responsibility sexually," she remarked, casually and completely unaffected by my obvious attempt to goad her. "Just as I have to look after my own," she suddenly added, and my cheeks flushed as I realized whom she was referring to. Touché. She had got me.

"I'll wait here for your dirty things. Jez will have them washed and then the two of you can decide later on tonight which of her clothing you can make your own." She held out a bag for me to put my current clothing in, making another reference to their being *dirty,* as well as another not-so-subtle remark about how strongly humans taint their apparel with their odors.

As I removed my clothes I realized that she had once again arranged things where I was before her naked, and I wondered if there was anything more to that. But she didn't appraise my body openly as she had the day before, and when I shoved the articles of clothing into the bag, she took them and left without any further comments and didn't wait to watch me dress as I thought she might.

It felt funny to walk out into the open air with that brief dress and not even a pair of panties underneath, but fortunately the air was not very chill, and eventually I even came to enjoy the sensation caused by the occasional breeze that strayed up past its hem. I went to the celebration early, knowing that the concept of arriving fashionably late would be lost on this crowd and figuring that I would offer my assistance to Cookie, who has been so good to me.

The first person I saw was of course Bill, who seemed to be waiting just for me, and I don't think that was simply in my imagination. Behind him were tables of food and a very special one of desserts and snacks, and almost every one of them covered in... chocolate!

"What are they trying to kill us?" I exclaimed, thinking I had discovered a new definition for "Death by Chocolate."

"No," he answered excitedly, and since I didn't recall him being that upset over the thought of never eating that wondrous delicacy again, I could only imagine that he was excited for my benefit. "I was misinformed, or rather I misunderstood. Chocolate *is* poisonous to us, but just as we are able to grow back missing limbs, we are also able to counter the effects of all poisons. Silver is still the only thing that can kill us. Chocolate just makes us extremely sick—perhaps even violently so—although just as with dogs it affects some worse than others. So on rare, special occasions, they allow us the choice—if we think it's worth it—to indulge, or simply sample it, at our own discretion. Personally I'd like to find out just what kind of effect it has on *me*, and I'm sure you are going to want to eat as much as you dare, for it may be a lo-o-ong time before it's offered again. I had never seen them offer it before, not that I've been here *that* long. So shall we?"

He began heading for the table but held back when I told him that I would rather save dessert for *after* the meal. I didn't want any nausea—or worse—ruining my enjoyment of this event—which hadn't even begun yet—and preferred to save such experiments for the end of the night.

Bill introduced each Dingo as they arrived, and I was pleased, and more than a little surprised, to discover that they were all very good-natured and friendly, and apparently like Bill they held no resentment regarding their present condition. I asked about the Dingo children, none of whom were in sight, and was told that they would have their own party, and that this one was for the adults. Apparently the behavior of the adults would not be appropriate for the youths, although I did see Mackey, who was arguably a youth himself, despite his special consideration as the pack's future alpha.

A blonde woman roughly my age seemed to be very taken with me. After Bill introduced her, she hung around and rarely took her eyes off me. Her smile was that of an infatuated schoolgirl, and she seemed to be forever on the verge of breaking out in giggles. I tried discretely to ask Bill what her deal was, which wasn't too easy with her constant presence and close vigil, but he waved off my concern and told me that she was harmless and did that to every new female initiate. He told me that she was sweet and eager to make friends, but usually put people off by being *too* eager, and her attempts at finding a new "best friend" were deemed irritating by most. Her name was Samantha, and when I told her my name she was effusive in her compliments: "Oh, what a lovely name! It suits you. You're very beautiful; have you thought about being one of Jez's girls? No? Good. The competition's fierce enough as it is. If *you* came along, everyone would want you and none of us would ever get any work... No, of course we wouldn't be glad about that. We take pride in our work and enjoy it... Well, maybe not every girl feels that way... but they *should* if they were true to their community."

Great. A regular cheerleader for the werewolf way of life. But I couldn't dislike her. My Psych training informed me that she was probably very lonely in her old life, with few if any friends, and would have readily embraced this culture, seeing its close-knit community as an opportunity for fitting in, primarily because there would be no choice in the matter—she would *have* to be accepted by the pack.

Bill basically ignored her, as did the rest. I hate to admit it, but I even forgot that she was there after only a few minutes. She may have been within a few feet from me at all times, but I took no more notice to her after our initial discussion than I would a nearby lamp. And I felt awful about it, but to be honest the last thing I wanted right now was another person trying to implant herself into my life. So I let myself get caught up in whatever Bill had to say, and eventually I did notice that she was no longer nearby. She had placed herself among the rest of Jez's girls, but still seemed to stand out as though she were all by herself. The fact that nobody spoke much more than the occasional sentence to her helped enforce that impression.

And I hate to admit it now, but all it took was a turn of my head in anyone else's direction for me to completely forget the poor girl and her predicament. I was aware of this then too, and I was about to go over and force myself to tolerate her attentions when I was mercifully interrupted by Jez, who held out my arms for better inspection and decided: "Aryana's choice, am I right?" She looked at me with a smirk and a sidelong glance, and I laughed and admitted that it was indeed she who chose my attire for the evening. She took me by the arm and steered me toward her establishment so that I could pick out my personal wardrobe, joking as we walked. "So I hear that you would like some change of clothing in your room so that you don't have to walk around naked as nature intended. Oh, you humans, you've got such funny ways." Her perpetual good-natured smile assured me that she was not to be taken serious, and I laughed and enjoyed being in this larger-than-life female's presence. "Don't worry, you won't miss anything good back at the party. It'll take a while for the wine to flow and the wolves to howl. You can't consider one of our parties underway as long as we're all in human form."

I must have showed a little panic over that statement, for she suddenly patted me and assured me that I had nothing to worry about, that they may turn into drunk wolves, but they'll never act like a wild Dingo during a full moon. And she amended that statement by informing me that the wine and other alcohols had little effect on them and didn't last for very long either, as their body would act against the effects of the brain cell–killing liquid as it would against anything injurious, reminding me of what Bill said about the chocolate. When I asked how they were able to put Dingoes to sleep if our body fights off the effects of drugs, she sighed and admitted that the potions they use occasionally don't do their job, and that they are constantly trying new elements from nature that would do the trick better. I found this disheartening, fearing my first night of change, but she assured me that most of us don't have to worry, and that sleeping draughts aren't fought off by our bodies the way life-threatening things are.

She then proceeded to tell me a little about the revelries that went on the night before while the Dingoes were all either sleeping or thrashing about out of control. I was made privy to certain indelicate matters that I doubted were meant for my ears, but apparently gossiping about its own members is a big part of community life among the *Canis sapiens*. As it turned out, I already figured prominently among their idle chatter. My friendship with Bill was widely discussed, as well as propositions of what they would do to us should the unmentionable happen between us. She cast another one of those sideways looks at me and, still smiling, inquired about it. "So, uh, is there anything to that? You don't have to worry about me. I know how to zip my mouth shut when I hafta. You can tell me. Are you in love?"

"I've only just met the man," I exclaimed, to which she responded, satisfied, to herself: "She's in love."

We arrived at her brothel, and we went upstairs so that I could pick out the things that both fitted and appealed to my tastes. Fortunately not all of Jez's wardrobe consisted of the type of clothing that Aryana chose to wear, and some were quite demure and respectable, as a matter of fact. We had armfuls of clothes with us as we continued on to my cabin, and after depositing them on my bed I immediately led the way toward the door. When I noticed that she had hesitated, I turned and looked at her questioningly.

"Aren't you going to change before going back to the celebration?" she asked hesitantly.

"No, why should I?" I replied with the utmost confidence. "Aryana is not the only one who can get away with wearing clothing like this. Do you think I want to let her think that I am not as daring as her?"

Jez beamed in appreciation of my determination, and I took it that Aryana was not the most beloved bitch in the pack.

I sauntered — practically strutted — back to the Social Center with Jez at my side, and in the time we were gone, the number of party attendees had grown to the point where it looked like the whole community had turned out — and given their lust for living it up, they probably all had. I had barely returned when I immediately regretted my decision to not change clothes. Mackey, who was currently entertaining two of his young male companions with stories of some adventurous escapade that was most likely exaggerated, leered at me and barked at me in a mocking way. "Hey Teach!" he called out. "So you wanna see just how much of a Coyote ol' Mackey can be? Oh, wait, 'old Mackey' is just that — *too old* for you. You seem to like 'em much younger, don't you, like that Dingo whelp who's been seen leaving your room earlier today?" He then punctuated his comments with vulgar motions that did their job to prompt hearty laughter from his two companions, as well as anyone else near enough to witness.

I quelled my outrage and attempted to pass haughtily by, but after a couple of long steps I yelped in surprise, realizing too late that in a dress as short as this—and with no underwear for protection—my steps should have been much smaller, with my legs closer together. Somehow my vagina was being tickled, and when I looked down I saw that Mackey was bending over with pants slightly lowered, extending his canine tail from his human form's backside, and wiggling it up my dress. The laughter seemed to erupt into a deafening roar, and I struggled to ignore it and keep my dignity, hiding my mortification only marginally.

Jez snatched the tail and yanked on it hard, pulling Mackey off-balance and causing him to emit a brief and very canine yelp of his own. "So you want a piece of *tail*," she said, gripping the offending tail and playing with the fur at its tip. "I'm not sure yer quite wolf enough for a lady like that. And as fer me..." She must have been making some obscene gestures with his tail that I didn't catch, stunned as I still was with my previous molestation. I knew that she had it firmly in her grip, and that our audience was enjoying her taunts and her actions immensely. "Oh, Mackey baby," she concluded, making a tsk sound as she paused, "you can't even keep your tail erect for me." Amid the howls of amusement, Jez gently prodded me with a hand, letting me know that I had an opportunity to slip away and should take it. Seeing that even Mackey was enjoying Jez's attentions, I quietly moved on and re-joined my Dingo friends, who had all seemed to congregate to the same set of tables and park benches, the same ones they were at when I left them. Taking a seat next to Bill (which I'm sure he did his best to keep unoccupied), I remarked about the segregation and asked if we were the equivalent of "wallflowers."

"No, there'll be plenty of intermingling as the night progresses, but perhaps none that you would want to participate in," he responded.

"I think I'm going to regret coming to this," I commented, my anxiety showing.

"I certainly hope not," he immediately replied. "I was hoping we'd get to know each other better tonight."

As gently as I could, I said, "Bill, you know we can't..."

"I don't mean *that*. Trust me, I don't wanta get killed either. Rules are rules, and golden ones can't be broken," he began, with a trace of disappointment in his tone. "No, what I mean is... well, we're gonna be in this community for an awful long time—God willing," he interrupted himself, *knocking wood* on the table in front of us. He also averted his eyes, which told me that what he was saying was coming from the heart. "It'd just be nice to have a close, human friend here, who I might have things in common with," he said, measuring his words carefully, then quickly adding, "like our writing!"

I patted his hand, telling him that I understood, then quickly pulled my hand back as Jez approached.

"You won't have to worry about Mackey anymore tonight. Besides, he's gonna be with Jack most of the time, so he'll be kept busy." She was about to leave us Dingoes to our business, when she leaned back in and beamed as if she were about to reveal a juicy secret that we would all want to know. And it was much appreciated, at least by Bill and me, who were apparently the only ones whom it applied to. She told us, "Party all you want tonight, folks; school's out tomorrow." She then left us with a wink and a twirl, dashing off to pull some unsuspecting wolf up to join her on her imaginary dance floor.

"All right!" Bill cheered. "Now I can relax and have fun with the girls all night."

Confusion knitted my brow, which furrowed deeper as his words exposed a mysterious revelation. "All the Dingoes are girls," I said flatly. "Well, except you."

"And don't forget Cookie's brother," Bill amended. "But yes, it does seem to be that ninety percent of Dingoes bitten are of the female persuasion. Makes you wonder just what goes into the decision-making process, doesn't it? I mean, they *say* that they try to keep our numbers down and only bite out of necessity and when given no other choice, but apparently sex and appearance play into the equation as well. Just look at all the attractive Dingoes among us, almost all of whom work for Jez in her house of pleasure. Seems to me that they just like keeping their kennels stocked with pretty, young sex slaves. Opinions?"

He kept his tone so that his words were just for me, but I couldn't answer him, for I was looking at the others, reevaluating the things told to me by Jack and considering Bill's observation and disturbing theory. It may not have been upsetting to him, a man, but the thought of beautiful women in danger of being abducted for the sole purpose of becoming sex slaves is an old fear for women, no doubt going as far back as the beginning of time. I can recall stories of the infamous white slave market and women being shipped overseas, but to have *this* debatably worse threat exist out there for all females to worry about made the world an even bleaker place, and life in it more nightmare-filled. I felt like I was in a living, breathing, all-too-real Grimm's fairy tale. I gazed at each of the girls, and when I came to Samantha I quickly looked away, knowing she would try to catch my eye in hope of an invitation. I of course hated myself for doing that.

"Still... " Bill began, "one may consider us fortunate. After all, who wouldn't want to be genetically enhanced?"

"Enhanced?" I blurted out.

"Sure. Eyesight improved. All other senses heightened. The ability to grow back a body part, including organs damaged beyond repair. Immunity to diseases and tumors. Never to worry about cancer or AIDS again..."

"Okay, okay, I get your message," I interrupted, still not wanting to see the silver lining and preferring to hold onto my loathing and despair.

"And from what I hear, there's a certain little something you no longer need worry about eleven months out of the year."

"All right!" I exclaimed, then forced myself to calm down, for even I couldn't explain my behavior at that moment. Then I kindly remarked, "Perhaps I'll feel that way once I've experienced some of these things firsthand. As it is, I still feel no different." He accepted that concession and nodded, making no reference to my sudden outburst and staying quiet to let me steer the conversation in whatever direction I felt comfortable with.

"I need a chocolate," I finally said. "Shall we?"

"Let's," he replied in turn, and we headed for the goodies table that both enticed and terrorized me at the same time. I sampled one morsel cautiously, Bill watching intently for my reaction to it. It was predetermined without saying that I would be the guinea pig, as I was not yet a full-fledged Dingo physically, and would thus have a better tolerance to the poisonous delicacy. When he saw that I not only survived the treat without incident, but found it to be exquisite, he tried one as well, and when he too had no adverse reaction to it, we both picked among the sweets for our favorites, being careful to not overdo it.

We returned to the table and the same seats we had recently vacated when we noticed the larger number of dancers that had followed Jez's lead and were hoofing it up on the makeshift dance floor. He looked at me, and his eyes seemed to ask a question, to which I responded with my own eyes. *Care to dance? Love to!* And so without a word being spoken we got up again as one and headed out to join the dancers, but keeping a safe distance from them, as we were not *Canis sapiens* and didn't know how accepted our presence would be. But we were greeted with smiles, and Jez turned out to still be among them, her presence alone making us feel more comfortable.

The night grew darker and the campfires grew fiercer, providing little-needed heat and much-needed light for the festivities. I don't know if it was because of the darkness, or because it was hard to see beyond the flames of the bonfires, but either there weren't as many people here anymore or I simply wasn't able to see them. Either way, it helped relax me to not feel the eyes of so many wolves upon us. I knew that in the dark of night many would take their revelries out into the woods in canine form, and that was just fine with me, so long as they stayed out there in the woods and away from the fires and the food and dancing. Less of them around was better, as far as I was concerned, and I was sure my Dingo sisters would feel the same way and not remain stuck to their seats like glue once our numbers approached, or even surpassed, the number of true werewolves nearby. A glance over at the "Dingo section" seemed to prove my point; it was empty. But if they weren't there, where were they, as I had not seen one of them dancing in our area?

I could not consider this further, because suddenly Bill faltered on his feet. When I looked into his face, I could see how his attention was elsewhere; he didn't even seem to know I was there anymore. His face was pale, and he stared blankly in front of him, seeing nothing, as he fought back an obvious urge to heave. I recognized this look immediately, as I had seen enough friends overdo it with liquor to the point where they were too sick to acknowledge anything beyond their own bodily sensations. But I had not witnessed Bill drink nearly enough to make himself sick, and I didn't think he could drink himself into such a stupor in the short while that I slipped away with Jezebel. If he had, there would have been evidence of this when I had returned, but he had been as clear and sober as I was, and he didn't slur his words or stumble even slightly as we walked over to the choc—Oh my God, the chocolate! I hurriedly led him to some hedges at the side wall of the Social Center, where I didn't think any partygoers would stray, and helped him to his knees so that he could purge his system of the toxins that had finally affected him.

When it happened, it was worse than anything I had ever seen before. No human being has ever vomited the way he had that night. In addition to the fluid that one normally expels, there was blood and pieces of what I imagined to be inner organs, and by the way his body distorted and by the look of pain expressed on his face, I don't doubt that I was not far from the truth. It literally lasted at least five full minutes, but it didn't end there. After he had heaved his last, he lay still, on his side, eyes squeezed shut, not moving or wanting to be touched. His body was making strange sounds and through his shirt his stomach could be seen lurching and shivering. After another five minutes of this, his eyes relaxed but remained closed, and he still stayed on his side, but the violent actions of his body no longer seemed as fierce. In fact, they began dwindling to little more that the occasional spasm.

In that time I looked around to see if anyone was watching. At the edge of the woods I could see Samantha looking right at me, her expression blank. She was on her hands and knees between bushes, and I almost didn't see the wolf perched on her back, partly due to the darkness and the pitch black color of the animal, and partly because of the foliage they were hiding out in for their act. Her head was jerking from the force of the thrusts behind her, and I wondered about the pitiable look on her face. Was it there because she was truly unhappy in this life she was raving so much about, or was it that *she* was actually pitying *us* for what *we* were currently going through?

I looked down at Bill, and in my imagination I could picture his internal organs re-forming, replacing the ones that I had imagined were being expelled from his body previously. I do believe that this was exactly what was happening to him, and after a few more minutes he opened his eyes and held out a hand to me, which I clasped between my own. He reached out further and wiped away tears that I had no idea were staining my cheeks and the soft, delicate skin beneath my eyes.

When he was ready to stand, we stepped cautiously back to the table we had sat at earlier—but which felt like days ago—expecting all eyes to be upon us, but in fact no one even noted our return, engaged as they were in what I can only describe as an orgy of fur and flesh. I recalled how this was considered an adults-only party, and now I knew why. Between what I just went through with Bill and what I was currently witnessing, I decided that for me the party was over. So I asked Bill if he wished to return to his cabin and if he needed help getting there, and when he responded in the affirmative to both inquiries, I happily led him away from the jubilation.

I helped Bill home, which took a considerable amount of time, given he could only take a few steps before pausing again, fighting the urge to double over. But when we entered his room he resisted no longer, and he collapsed onto his bed without a word or even a glance in my direction. I believe that in his pain he had actually forgotten I was even there, or that he had even been accompanied by anyone the whole walk back, despite the fact that he had leaned on me the entire way. His eyes were squeezed shut again, and his stomach was working its strange magic, leaving me to conclude that the walk had agitated the healing process. I tugged at his shirt to lift it from his body, and he peeked through parted lids and seemed to take a moment before recognizing me. Then he lifted his body a bit, but not without obvious discomfort, to assist me in my attempts. I helped roll him to the center of the bed and managed to free the loose top sheet without needing to readjust him much. I yanked off his sneakers and socks, and before pulling the sheet over him I debated whether I should remove his pants as well, deciding I would leave it up to him. I reached out and unbuttoned the top of his jeans and figured that if he stopped me I would leave them on him, and if he lifted again I would peel them off. I slowly unzipped his fly and watched closely for either indication of how to proceed, and none to my surprise—but slightly to my dismay—he indeed lifted his hips for me to continue. My dismay was not because I *didn't* want to take off his pants but because I *did* want to, although certainly not under these conditions. And what if he happened to subscribe to the canine way of not wearing any underpants?!

His body quivered from the exertion of holding himself up and the accompanying pain, so I hurriedly removed his pants, both looking and trying not to look at the same time. Fortunately—yet also disappointingly—he was indeed wearing underpants, which were wet and clinging to his body, as he had broken out in a sweat all over. Seeing this I pulled the sheet up around him and lay my body over his—on top of the sheet!—to give him added warmth. I could feel the lurching and spasms as his body attempted to heal itself, and suddenly he pushed me up with alarming strength and rolled to the side to vomit fiercely once again. This proved to be the final violent act in this regenerating process for him on this evening, and he rolled back into a deep sleep, leaving me to clean up after him and then return to my position on top of him, providing body heat. I knew there were guards watching us, as there surely must have been the whole night, but I no longer cared about that. *Canis sapiens* be damned! This wasn't sex! It may have been interpreted as an act of love—no, it most certainly *was* an act of love, and caring—but it still was not in violation of their precious Golden Rule!

In the morning I awoke to find Aryana standing beside the bed, looking down on us. I didn't know what to expect from her, standing there quietly with a cup in her hands, and when I failed to say anything to her for a full minute, she decided to break the silence herself, but surprisingly made no mention of our indiscretion.

"He needs to drink this," she informed me. I sat up and began to reach out uncertainly for the cup, but she stopped me by saying, "He's my responsibility. Thank you for what you have done so far, but I will take over from here." This wasn't said with any hint of sincerity, but after I raised myself from his still-sleeping form—a difficult act, considering how I did not want to break the connection to him—she favored me with an explanation that she didn't *have* to provide, but graciously did nevertheless: "He would best be attended to by someone familiar with what is happening to him inside."

I was shocked. By giving me a reason, and not mentioning the way we were when she found us, Aryana was actually being *nice* to me. She must have really been grateful for all I did for him that night, while she was off doing God-knows-what with God-knows-whom. I recalled that Jack was nowhere to be seen the entire celebration, and also remembered Jez's words about Mackey being kept busy somewhere with Jack, obviously away from the revelries. So what *was* Aryana doing last night, and just *whom* was she doing it with? I had not seen her the whole time — and was immensely glad for that, so as not to spoil my time — but with them in wolf form I would not have been able to recognize *anyone*, so she could have easily been in front of me the whole time, or part of that mound of squirming bodies that I saw engaged in carnal canine delights.

Perhaps she had something to hide and, not realizing that I could not possibly possess any dirt on her, thought that by being nice to me today I would not tell Jack something that perhaps I knew. In any case, I appreciated anything that would keep her from acting like a bitch to me (no pun intended) for as long as was humanly, or caninely, possible.

I went to my own cabin, and it wasn't until I got inside and sat down on a chair that I realized how my hands were shaking. I crashed down on my bed instead and opted for more sleep, and didn't wake up until the afternoon when I heard a timid knock on my door. It was little Ricky Hasselhoff, checking in on me since he hadn't seen me in school today. I told him that I thought school was out today, due to the partying of the teachers the night before, and he informed me that Jez ran the children's celebration during school time, and he was disappointed to not see me there.

I apologized to him and told him how I wished I were there, and would have made sure to be there if I only knew about it in time. And I also told him how I had to take care of a sick friend through the night, leaving me exhausted and shaken in the morning, not exactly the best shape to enjoy a party in anyway. He nodded quietly, still looking down but not seemingly upset. I think he considered my reason to be a good one and forgave me.

"So tell me all about it," I said, inviting him to take a seat on the chair while I leaned forward eagerly from my bed, hanging on every word. I was happy to learn that he did indeed have a good time without me nevertheless, and that none of the other children picked on him or put him in a cage or anything. I supposed that was only because the Dingoes were the guests of honor, and didn't get my hopes up that their treatment of him will have improved or still be so respectful by the next day.

When he left a few hours later I was feeling much perkier and chipper, eager to see how the rest of the Dingoes had fared from last night's events—especially my favorite one, who I hoped was well enough to go to dinner with me. But when I knocked on Bill's door Aryana answered it, her body blocking the entrance. "He's not ready yet," was all she said, coolly but still without her usual rudeness. I was about to ask if I could at least look in on him to see how he was doing, but she closed the door firmly, not giving me the opportunity to even speak.

I went to the Social Center and talked with Cookie about all that transpired. She was sympathetic, sisterly, everything I could have hoped for. She fed me well and assured me that the next day would be a better one. And she was right. Bill actually paid me a visit before class, waking me up and then waiting outside as I dressed so that he could walk with me to the school lodges, after first stopping by the Social Center for some grub to take with us.

"That's not the kind of impression I wanted to make on you," he said with an attempt at humor, although his smile was forced and I could see that he was being more honest than witty. "I ruined the whole celebration for you."

"Are you kidding," I said. "With all that was going on there, I was looking for an excuse to get away." My attempt at humor was more successful, and his smile became more genuine as he realized what was probably happening at the party as I dragged him home, for he was too out of it to have noticed any of it at the time.

"Glad to be of service," he joked back. "Anytime you need me to cause a diversion by swallowing poison or takin' a bullet, you just let me know, all right?"

He was completely healed, or so he said, although I detected a bit of a catch in his voice every now and then, and his gait lacked the usual spring to his step. When I entered my classroom, Mackey was beaming at me from his seat, and I felt uneasy wondering what he had to be so pleased with himself about. I did a perfunctory inspection to make sure there were no tacks on my seat or anything else on or around my desk that would prove to be a booby trap of his, and carefully sat when I came up empty.

"I hope you all had a good time yesterday," I began. "But now it's time to get to work. I believe a discussion on the Internet might be a good place to start with today..."

Mackey had his hand up, and reluctantly I asked him to speak what was on his mind.

He came to the front of the class in order to address them, just as I had made him do last time, and said, "I would like to share with you something that happened two nights ago, while all you pups were tucked soundly in bed."

No. He couldn't be planning to bring up our little incident at the beginning of the party here to all the class. Could he? I had to stop him, to point out the inappropriateness of what he was about to say, especially given his audience—*my* class—who were required to look upon me with nothing but respect. "Mackey, I don't think they need to hear about what went on at an event that they were too young to attend."

But he was brushing aside my comment. "This has nothing to do with your little Dingo party," he said dismissively, and with unveiled disdain. "It's about what Jack and I were doing while you were all..." he searched for a word that wouldn't offend his young listeners, "indulging yourselves."

Oh. This I hadn't expected. Even I was now curious and wished to hear about this tidbit of information, despite the source and my feelings toward him.

He began: "In the nearby village there's this ATM machine that has a bad reputation for being in a spot that's too out-of-the-way, thus making it dangerous for its users to take out money from. Well we learned about this old man who is not in the best of health, who stubbornly goes to this machine all the time. Now, there's a gang that has been expanding its territory to the point where this machine falls within their land. So when this old man next goes to withdraw money, he's bound to be hit, right? That's exactly what we expected two nights ago, since he goes there the same day every week, and, sure enough, they hit him—hard—and took whatever money he had on him."

He turned to me to explain something, "As you should know by now, obtaining money from the dead is how we get by, so we have scouts who are good at watching for opportunities like this and whose purpose it is to predict the best possibilities for a major score." He turned his attention back to the class. "Well, their predicted outlook for the night was high, and so they sent word back to us, and Jack decided that this mission would be mine. A test, really. So when we got there this guy was already taken care of—" He must have sensed my confused expression, because he glanced over at me to clarify. "Dead. He was already dead. He didn't have a dime left on him, but he did have his ATM card—the gang didn't think to take that from him; they know they'll never hit upon the right PIN number to get any more money out."

His excitement was contagious, but I was still stuck on thoughts of that poor old man whom they had knowingly let die at the hands of a murderous street gang.

"I sniffed around the body and then turned my hands human so that I could extract his card from his wallet. Then I took it to the machine and, keeping only my hands in human form, inserted the card and entered the PIN number and withdrew the geezer's entire life savings. A major coup!" he cheered, rousing the class's enthusiasm, but leaving me with my mouth gaping open. "How did I learn the PIN number, you may ask?" he said, toying with his audience. A few played along, asking him "How, how?"

"With this," he said, pointing to his nose. "When I was sniffing around the body, I paid special attention to his fingertips, the oils his skin produces, the personal scent of his skin. Then, at the ATM machine, I just sniffed for the four keys that he had touched, tried them a few times in assorted orders, and hit upon the right one on the fifth try!" He said this with a great deal of pride, as I unsuccessfully tried to compute the total number of outcomes that one could obtain from four individual numbers jumbled in distinct, different orders.

"And it wasn't all random guessing either," he went on boastfully. "They say that with a lot of experience you could tell exactly what order the buttons were pressed. Even if he pushed the same one twice! And I'm telling you, I could slightly sense a difference in how strong the remaining scent was, whether he pushed one a second earlier or later, which one was first or last, whether..." He continued singing his own praises, although I found his claims to be too far-fetched and rooted in exaggeration to be thoroughly impressed. "Given enough practice, I believe I too will be able to get it right on the first try, every time, in say... a year or two."

He smiled over at me, and was a bit confused by my stunned expression, which he could tell was not in appreciation of his talents. "So you're saying," I began, "you knew he was about to be killed, you allowed it to happen in the manner predicted, and then you stole his money, to add insult to injury." His expression lost some of the smugness, as he struggled to retain his self-possessed smirk. "*And you're probably on camera doing it*," I continued, "as that machine no doubt has a camera fitted to it for just such purposes!"

"All they have on tape is a wolf going up to the keypad and leaving with money, if they can even convince themselves that that is what they are actually seeing. This isn't a first time for us, just a first for me. You humans will invent any kind of explanation, in search of something that is *rational,* even when the truth is staring you right in the face. Wolves have been caught on tape doing all sorts of unbelievable things, and it is simply described as that: unbelievable. Surely you've heard stories of a human baby being lost and then sheltered by wolves, only to be returned to its family unharmed?"

"That was one of you?" I asked, but he wouldn't give me a reply.

He returned to his seat, taunting: "You tell me. Was it an actual wolf, doing the *unbelievable,* or was it one of us, doing nothing so extraordinary? I'll just wait here for your *rational* answer."

So, not everything about this day was better, as was predicted, but at least he didn't brag about what he did to me at the beginning of the celebration.

"Oh," he stage-whispered to me from his seat, "about that thing you thought I was going to mention up there before, I already brought it up yesterday."

Great. Getting better by the minute.

. . . . .

That afternoon, Ricky visited again, and I was glad to see that this was becoming a regular after-school activity for him, and both of us enjoyed it. And it was actually beneficial for both of us, serving to keep him away from his tormentors and in the presence of someone who cares, and helping me keep my interests at a G-rating, evoking motherly instincts rather than sexual ones, as in the company of another Dingo male in this community — and I don't mean Cookie's brother.

This continued the next day, and I expected and looked forward to his sudden knocking at my door on a daily basis. He became much more comfortable around me, as evidenced by his unsolicited browsing of the contents of my handbag, which I didn't mind and didn't even call attention to, much less reprimand him for.

"Can I have this?" he asked, interrupting me as I went about my business reading essays I had assigned the children the day before. Sometimes we didn't even have to speak; just each other's presence was comfort enough for us both, and so I barely turned my head to see what he was referring to as I mumbled a sound halfway between a "Hmm?" and an "Uh-huh." But I did glimpse enough, and I suddenly jumped up with an exclamation of fear and surprise as I saw him hold out that damn Hershey's Kiss candy that I had never gotten rid of. With thoughts of Bill's experience still strong in my mind, and figuring that Ricky's frail young body would be sorely affected by even so minor a piece of chocolate as this, my terrorized response was entirely justified, but when he dropped it to the floor in his own surprise, his face suddenly expressed a pain which I couldn't account for.

His other hand was in a fist, clenched close to his body, and he hesitantly held it out and relaxed his fingers to reveal what had caused him such discomfort. As his fingers uncurled and his palm flattened out, I could see a shiny little object and an even tinier drop of blood. And then I realized what the object was, and my terror multiplied as I froze, unsure of how to handle this emergency. The tiny object was my discarded earring. The one made of silver. Piercing his palm deeply.

I watched in horror as the wound opened, erupting like a volcano, with blood and other fluids gushing out and cascading over the sides of his hand and running down his arm like molten hot lava. And after a moment of staring in disbelief at the wound, Ricky suddenly registered the pain, and it was as if it actually *was* molten hot lava pouring over his tender young flesh. His mouth formed a scream that froze on his face, and suddenly he seemed to be getting smaller and thinner, and it was no illusion. His skin was peeling in parts as if he had been sunburned, and wherever this happened the exposed flesh underneath appeared to be melting and dripping off his body. I finally found my voice, and scrambled to the doorway screaming for assistance, yelling words like "Help! Silver! Help!" until numerous *Canis sapiens* rushed in to assay the scene for themselves.

They rushed to the body and led me away from it a bit, but I could still see the decaying and dissolving, and for a moment I thought that his still-seeing eyes locked onto mine, his mouth still forming that soundless scream, leaving me to wonder if his look was accusing me or pleading with me to somehow help him as I always had before. Then the look was gone, because the face had sunken in and the head collapsed in on itself, the rest of the body shriveling right there on the floor of my home. Jack was suddenly next to me, holding my arm as if to steady me, and placing his other hand to the side of my face to turn my gaze away from the awful spectacle. His hand fell away then, and I snapped my head right back to the sight, but everyone was staring solemnly at me instead, the one closest to the child's remains holding aloft the offending silver earring. The murder weapon. I was led by Jack out of the room, and I knew that I could never set foot back inside, for the memories would haunt me forever.

. . . . .

Jack led me to the Social Center and sat me down at a table, gesturing for Cookie to bring me some food without saying a word. I sat stunned, still not feeling the full extent of the grief that would soon hit me—and hard. Jack was speaking, and I was only half-consciously picking up on what he was saying, though I made no reply and just sat there staring ahead. A TV from the game room to the side was on and I was positioned in such a way that I could see it, so I used it as a focal point and watched without really seeing it. I only registered enough to know that the news was on.

"That was bad," he said simply. "It's not usually like that; like I said, we try to be humane. Even when we have to take down a Dingo who's gone wild, our bullets—not true silver bullets like your Lone Ranger carries, but ordinary bullets with a small trace amount of argentum in 'em—is enough to do the trick without that much of a show." I could sense him pause and drop his head, floundering for an explanation. "You see, problem is... here the child wasn't in werewolf form. If he was, the silver would've triggered a reversal and his body would've gone limp in its transformation back to human form before disintegrating—with the person subdued and effectively unconscious for it! It's not like how you saw it just now. That was..." Again he was stuck on what to say. "I've never even seen anything like that before."

Although not visibly evidenced from my countenance, his words were appreciated. He was actually showing me a human side to him, and it was a welcome change from his usual gruff exterior. I also appreciated the severity with which he treated the Dingo boy's death. There was a concern there that I did not expect for a Dingo, and whether it was more for the boy's tragedy or out of sympathy for what I was going through, I was inwardly thankful, although like I said I didn't show it.

"It also must have gone straight into a vein," he kept reasoning, trying to make sense of the extent of the death throes. "Sometimes our bullets don't hit any major organ or artery and the person slowly changes and dies a nice slow death, asleep and untroubled. Or maybe it has to do with his age, being so young and with such a shorter system of veins and organs so much closer to each other..." I began tuning him out, for he was simply rambling on at this point. "I mean, the end result is the same. There's not much of a body left worth identifying, and certainly no wound to suggest an explainable cause of death. And thus no one's ever been able to make the connection or get any practical evidence of the existence of werewolves in all the time that..."

"Ms. Journal's car has been discovered a mere eight blocks from her apartment, without any visible signs of damage or of a break-in.

And though no one can say for sure how long the car has been sitting there, the police have declared that she has now been surely missing for forty-eight hours and can be considered a missing person. Their count is determined based on the point when her monthly rent was last delivered to her landlord's door..." What was this? I was staring at a photo of myself that I clearly remembered being taken recently at my sister's engagement party, a photo only my mother has a copy of. And yet there it was on the television screen. My mouth dropped open, and eventually Jack noticed the change in my demeanor and ceased his one-sided conversation and looked at the screen too, quietly. The TV news reporter continued, but all I could see was an image in my mind's eye of my mother, distraught, obviously the one who reported my absence once she hadn't heard from me in a few days, for the evidence that it was her was staring me in the face on the screen. "If anyone should see this woman, please contact the local authorities immediately."

Somehow, amidst all that I was feeling, certain facts didn't elude my attention—bless my reporter's mind and attention to details! One was that, in order for me to be seeing this local news broadcast, I must not be far from my home, wherever we now were. Another was that they had returned my car relatively near to my home in an obvious attempt at misdirection for the police (I didn't even have to bring that one up for him to confirm), but another point puzzled me. "You paid my rent?"

"Ah, yes," he said, seemingly taken off-guard for a moment before answering. "It lets the trail go cold a bit longer before the police even begin looking into it. Plus there's the whole two-day delay before one can even be considered missing, so... it's not likely anyone is ever going to be able to track you down to us. Besides, they'll probably be searching for clues in the wrong location," he said smugly.

"Where you dropped off my car?" I asked, trying to chip away at his confident attitude. "You don't think they're going to fall for that and think that I'm anywhere near where you conveniently placed it, do you?"

But his behavior wasn't at all affected. "Well they're gonna have to start somewhere, aren't they?" he shot back. "And besides, it's not like you told anyone where you'd be, did you?" I was about to lie, but then held my tongue. "I thought not. Considering the subject matter, you were probably too embarrassed to admit to anyone what your new story was about, and perhaps you even made up something about where you were going that night. If you even spoke to anyone, that is. It's not like there's a man in your life, is there, or someone to check in with?" How could he know so much about me? "Don't worry, pussycat, no one's comin' for you. And what's it to us if we throw some money toward paying your rent. It's not like it's *our* money anyway. No skin off our tail."

He had a point there. Money meant nothing to them, and if they needed any they could just watch some old geezer get bumped off and then steal from his bank account, right? Probably steal the gold caps right out of their mouth if they had any teeth capped — My blood froze within me. Fillings. What about my silver fillings?!

I turned to Jack wide-eyed and stuttered, unable to even get the words out. "Mouth, teeth, fillings, silver — oh God!" was an approximation of the blubbering I spurted, but he made calming gestures with his hands and placed one on my shoulder, telling me "Those teeth will fall out during your transformation process, rejected by the body, and be replaced by new ones. You've nothing to fear. Have you got any really deep ones, perhaps from a root canal?" I shook my head in small, quick movements, still wide-eyed and unable to speak. "No? Good. Those might've caused some minor discomfort but then be rejected all the quicker. The worst you would get is a little sick. Apparently you have yet to feel any changes in your system, or so I've been told. Not unusual, considering the time of month. As the next full moon approaches, it'll happen."

Very comforting, I thought bitterly. A heaviness came over me and I realized that it was beginning to hit me, *really* hit me, and I asked Jack to take me home, then realized what was awaiting me there and asked him to find me a new home. He offered to take me to Jez's establishment where I could be with other girls and not be alone, but alone was what I wanted to be, so I declined the offer. I had to get out of the Social Center, away from werewolves and especially Dingoes, who were simply awaiting their own demise, like zombies who refuse or are too stupid to realize that they should just lie down and play dead. For that was how I saw all of us, once again, as victims who were dead but still walking, awaiting the day that the consequences of our murderers' vicious acts will come to fruition. I mourned for myself as well as for Ricky. Ricky... oh Ricky. I had to get out of there. If I didn't, I believed I would have fainted, something I never in my life thought I could possibly do until this month. So I rose and ambled off in a random direction, faltering and walking as if it were my first time, but Jack arrived at my elbow to steer me to the exit, and I made it out into the air where I could breathe again.

· · · · ·

I settled in on the opposite side of the School from where I had previously been staying, further from Bill's comforting presence, yet thankfully far from the nightmare I had wrought. The cabin was unfortunately identical to the one I had previously occupied, as they all probably are, and I was surrounded by familiar sights that helped me reenact that horrible scene in my mind over and over and over.

When my things were brought over to me, I was grateful to see my journal among them, but when I attempted to put to paper all that had just transpired, I found that the pain was too great and the events too fresh in my mind, a condition that is normally beneficial to a writer, but not this time. I wallowed, and was given time off from my duties at the school, allowing me time to continue my wallowing and my endlessly blaming myself for what had happened. If only I was a good little Dingo, I thought, none of this would have happened. Discard my chocolate and my silver, embrace my new way of life like that wretched girl Samantha, and bend over and stick my tail in the air so that any and all dogs could mount me and eventually make me so numb I would not know the difference or care...

And Ricky would still be alive.

This was how I spent most of the time since I wrote my last entry. Bill tried to visit me on occasion, but I wasn't ready to see him the first week. After that, I grudgingly let him in, and others, like Jez and Cookie, and even Samantha once. This past week was one of healing, and it is on that note that I close the worst chapter in my life.

SEVEN

"Hard to believe," I muttered. "Invincible as we are."

"But not immortal. You're confusing us with vampires," Bill replied.

We sat in the Social Center, awaiting a late lunch that Cookie was preparing. It was my first day out of my self-inflicted solitary confinement, but I couldn't stop dwelling on the same topic. It was as if I had emerged from a penitentiary, but would carry my sentence forever.

"Silver," I muttered some more. "We can grow back organs and limbs, live with perfect teeth and vision, never get sick or diseased. And our bodies can't survive a stupid, little, inconsequential thing as silver." I shook my head in disbelief. "I mean, what is *that* about?"

"It's not so astounding. I bet everything in nature has some little thing that can kill it. Look what salt does to a slug," Bill pointed out, ever the pragmatist.

"But slugs are simple organisms. They don't have the complex make-up that we do."

I thought that was a reasonable point, but Bill was not put off by it, and he countered with: "And the average human couldn't die by something as simple and inconsequential as eating a berry? Or a certain part of a certain fish? Or..."

"I get it," I interrupted, forced to concede victory to him in this matter.

Although I was once again out amongst the community, I was still relieved from my duties at school, pending my return to a more stable frame of mind (they do not approve of putting their impressionable young minds under the care of someone this frazzled, I suppose), and Jez had rearranged the classes back to the way they were before I came.

"We are, after all, still mortal," Bill concluded.

"Yeah, but with a shorter life-span."

"Not necessarily. If we are fortunate enough, and are able to survive multiple relocations without incident, we could live as long as any human could hope to. We don't suffer from the shorter life spans of the *Canis sapiens*. It's the one good human quality we retain."

"As opposed to all those 'good' werewolf ones?" I sarcastically remarked.

But if Bill had noticed my mocking tone, he did not acknowledge it and simply nodded his head. "Sure. And it would *have* to be that way. Otherwise a sixty-year-old man who was bitten would suddenly 'die of old age' long before his time."

"Just how far gone do we have to be before we cannot regenerate a body part?" I suddenly asked, jerking the conversation back to its original subject.

"Well, the limb or organ can basically reform in its entirety. I haven't witnessed much of this in my time here, but I've heard that if your heart was removed or blown away, your body would cease functioning for as long as it takes to grow a new one and continue normal life functions. Pretty amazing, huh? And of course, all the organs that are damaged from that would then begin healing as well. What I always wondered about was the brain. If someone had to grow back an entire brain, wouldn't that person become a new person? Without their original mind to recover all their life experiences, wouldn't they have a blank slate for a brain, with no memories of who they were, or even how to count or say the alphabet? They would have to start all over like a baby. That must be awful."

"Awful is a month with two full moons," I mumbled philosophically.

"Cookie's first month had that," Bill mentioned offhandedly.

"You mean that can happen?!" I cried out.

"Oh, yeah; that's called a blue moon, I think."

"You mean, like in the song?" I asked.

"Mmm-hmm," he answered uncertainly. "Or is it two *new* moons in a month."

"No, it's probably two full moons. That would make it 'blue' to any of us."

"That would make sense," Bill commented. "It is widely believed here that Dingoes might have been the first astronomers, that their need to understand and predict what was going to happen to them demanded their attention to the heavens, especially our closest celestial object."

Declining to offer a contradiction based on what I had heard about early astronomers, I accepted his explanation and sank into despair.

"It won't be so bad. You'll see," Bill said, attempting to cheer me up. "You just have to get through your first month, your first transformation. And once you've fully adapted, you'll experience a great lust for life, your senses heightened, everything in nature calling out for you to observe and revel in its beauty, or its scent, or its taste." Without intending to, he had entered forbidden territory again, as his last remarks took on a different meaning, which was clear from the look in his eyes. And from his next observation.

"Well, there is one drawback to our regeneration abilities." His change in topic would have taken me off-guard if it were not for my understanding of his feelings for me. "They can't just *neuter* us and then not have to worry about us procreating," he explained.

I hadn't thought of that. That's why they had to create their Golden Rule. Any attempt to surgically alter us so that we could not reproduce would not work. Their efforts would fail, as our body reverses the procedure and grows back whatever was removed. Thus forcing us to endure a more lasting torment: abstinence. Or an alternative that I was not ready to even entertain in my thoughts:

bestiality.

"Wow, you did it," I said dryly, to which Bill looked at me with a puzzled expression. "You managed to take my mind off silver and death, and... (I couldn't say his name just yet) for an entire minute."

"After all," he went on, ignoring what I said and sticking to his own topic, which apparently hounded him in the same way that mine did me, "that's the only reason why we—uh, Dingoes—can't engage in sexual activity. But when you consider that this Golden Rule was conceived at a time when birth control methods were nonexistent or ineffective at best, don't you think that—in a time when birth control is now pretty damn reliable—they should adapt this rule to suit the times? Maybe enforce birth control instead of simply restricting all contact. I mean, pills and spermicides and things like that don't work for *Canis sapiens*, I'm told, and so would probably not work on Dingoes either, but condoms—even doubled!—along with other precautions..."

He was blushing at that point and let his sentence trail off, his meaning fully understood—and, in this case, entirely agreed upon by me. Why couldn't we bring these canines into the twenty-first century? If they expect to join humanity, they're going to have to modernize their thinking and adapt some of their customs. "And have you ever expressed these opinions to our high exalted alpha?" I asked coyly.

"Well, I... never really felt the need to broach the subject before," he answered without meeting my gaze. "It didn't really matter that much to me before," he added with an extreme effort. But I wasn't about to let him off the hook on that one.

"And what's different now," I asked innocently, "that you are so bothered by it when you weren't before?" I nonchalantly looked around blankly. I realize now that I was shamelessly teasing him, but at the time my intentions were simply to be playful. After a brief silence I looked at him, and it wasn't until then, seeing him struggle to find the words while avoiding my eyes, that I realized the extent of his feelings for me. I felt awful and offered to mention his ideas to Jack when the time seemed appropriate.

A weight seemed to lift from his shoulders, and the smile he gave me was genuine and appreciative. "Just don't bring it up at this time of the month," he suggested, and then in answer to my confused look he added, "During a new moon. Haven't you noticed that everyone is a bit more skittish? The lack of a moon in the sky makes them uncomfortable and somewhat jittery. A real primal instinct that must go all the way back to their canine ancestry. Doesn't affect Dingoes, naturally, except that we try to stay out of their way during this time."

Cookie brought us our food and I suddenly had a thought. "What about Cookie?" When Bill failed to realize what I was asking him, I elaborated: "She's adorable; why haven't you ever wanted to...?"

"Oh." Bill thought for a moment and then said, "Cookie's... sorta like a sister. And before you ask, all of Jez's girls are pretty much reserved, if ya know what I mean. And I don't... (here, he looked around before continuing) really think I wanna spend any time with them after all the canine activity they're involved in. I know that sounds a bit hypocritical, but... I don't know. I guess it's just that I've never been with a prostitute before all this, and the idea of being with one just doesn't appeal to me." He whispered that last part.

"Gotcha," I said, allowing him to stop fumbling for an explanation he wasn't comfortable giving. "Perfectly understandable," I added, sympathizing with his parochial limitations, even though his weren't as strict as those I had set for myself upon entering their world.

"Of course, I could find a pretty Coyote and settle down," he said airily, in an obvious attempt at making me jealous. "Their history is full of stories about interspecies couples attempting to get by in the community. They've even got this popular play—I haven't seen it performed though—which is all about the trials of a young human-canine relationship... Sorta their version of Romeo and Juliet, I suppose."

"You could do that," I agreed, not giving in to the jealousy he hoped to provoke from me. "From what you've told me in the past, there are plenty of females in this community who would be up for it if they were not already spoken for."

"Well, for most of them, a little tryst with a Dingo may be an exotic diversion, but an emotional attachment with one is an entirely different thing," he mumbled, upset that I didn't play along the way he intended. "Besides, I'm not really interested in that kind of relationship."

"Relax," I said, patting his hand. "I already said I'd speak to Jack."

"How do you do it?" he asked, somehow seeming to already know where I stood on interspecies coupling. Perhaps Jez blabbed. Apparently that wouldn't be a first. "I know, you've only been here a couple of weeks, but when I think back to *my* first month here... Well, I guess I just don't have the willpower you do." He dropped his head, reminiscing and no doubt contemplating on the choices he made living in this community. I expect that, prior to his being bitten, getting together with women was not a problem for him and that he was rather sexually active. But for myself, going without for as short a stretch as this was nothing compared to past dry spells I'd lived through.

A few of my former students came into the Center, and one of them blanched upon seeing me in there; then he joined his friends at a table and made a concerted effort not to look my way. I commented on this to Bill, who looked over to see whom I was referring to.

"Paul," he said, and I recognized the name instantly. But I still didn't know why he would want to avoid me. "He's the one who bit Ricky." My eyes bulged out as I recalled this fact. "Came across Ricky in a wooded area and they started to play together. He enjoyed his company and—not knowing any better—he wanted to keep Ricky around as a playmate. Both of them should have been supervised at the time, but unfortunately both were alone and, neither old enough to know any better, Paul bit Ricky and turned him into one of us. He had to take Ricky in to learn responsibility for his actions. Probably resented it after a while because, even though Paul really liked him at first, he became one of Ricky's lead tormentors, as you witnessed yourself."

I looked over at Paul again, and even though he purposely wasn't looking, he could sense my gaze and was visibly disturbed by it. I looked back at Bill.

"It is believed that Jack is his sire," Bill remarked.

"Wait a minute. I've seen Paul with his parents. Jack—"

"No, no. You misunderstand. The concept of parents and parent*ing* are different among them. Many of the wolves here raise pups that were born from others. It's almost like a job. There are certain individuals better at raising children, and it is these whose role in the community is to do just that. A pup's mother and father are the ones who raise them; the actual birth parents are called their dam and sire. In most cases, the moms and pops here are also the dams and sires of their own children, but not in all. Certain wolves have duties—like in the case of the alpha—who are too busy with the concerns of the pack to be tied down with the concerns of one lone pup. In other cases, a dam may die in childbirth, or a sire may travel the land engaged in the business of survival of the species, like the Hyena or the 'government plants' you may have heard about. And so the pup is raised by another. It's a close-knit pack life, where everyone is considered family, so the importance we place on parenthood is defined differently by them."

"Yes, I recall our discussion about Jack's 'duties' in the pack. As 'breeding stock,' wouldn't you say?"

"Oh, more than that. He isn't just alpha of our pack; he currently holds the position of acting alpha for all the packs in this community—a very important position."

"Yes, yes. Like that of a president, right? Or a usurper."

"I know you don't approve, but consider how this system has been working for them for centuries, without the problems of infidelity that have plagued human relationships for just as long."

I didn't bother contradicting what he said based on what I had garnered from Jez during the night of the celebration, but I did point out that attempts by humans to live in this fashion have always ended poorly.

We ate in silence and then walked out into the crisp late-afternoon air, gazing up at where the moon usually was in the sky at this time of day. "After this, the waxing begins," Bill spoke, absentmindedly.

"The what?"

"Dingoes are said to be 'waxing' in the time between new and full moons. Ya know, just like the moon is in the waxing phase, as opposed to waning, which is from full to new. It's supposed to reflect our mental state during these times, waning meaning a time of cooling off where waxing apparently suggests nervousness and a building anxiety. But many Dingoes don't even experience it. I don't know any in our community that do."

"Oh." I looked once more at the empty spot in the sky and then continued walking toward my second home on this land.

"In fact, some even get overexcited during this time. Like myself. Heightened senses, more alert for some reason as the moon approaches full. A zest for living, an anticipation of some hunt that my body must want to go on while in wolf form, although frustrated by being chained up. It can be an exhilarating time, and maybe that's where they get the expression waxing from too."

I didn't know if there was sexual intonation implied there, but I was too put off by the expectation of how I would act during *my* 'waxing,' and I had a good idea which way it would go for me. We walked on, again in silence, which I found strange. Bill was always such a talker, there were never any gaps of uncomfortable silence like this. But when I stole the occasional glance over at Bill, he was very relaxed, and even content. The silence wasn't uncomfortable for him; he was simply enjoying a stroll out in nature with me, his 'gal.' And once I realized that, the silence wasn't so bad anymore. I had always felt that he was trying too hard and talking too much anyway. This was actually much better. And I had to admit that I enjoyed being out on a stroll with him too. The weather was beautiful, the setting was idyllic, the company was enchanting. If it weren't for the true reason behind our presence in this locale, it would have been the stuff dreams are made of. A sudden recollection of one particular dream involving the two of us in a similar setting made me blush, which he fortunately did not notice, and then another feeling took over and I could not deny what it meant.

When we arrived at my new home, he stopped at the door as per custom, but this time I told him that there would be no harm in his coming inside. "They can watch us through the window just as easily," I said. When he hesitated, I added, "You've been inside before." This was true, although that was only because I would not leave my room and had to have everyone cater to me, bringing me food and conversation, amidst attempts at getting me to reemerge into society. Now that I had reemerged, it was natural for things to revert to their original design, but I didn't want it to. He stepped uncertainly through the door behind me, glancing around nervously to see who was noticing and what their reaction would be, and once inside I closed it, trapping him between my body and the door.

"Shh. Right here is the hardest spot for them to observe from outside without actually pressing against the window," I told him, which automatically prompted him to shoot a nervous glance over at the window. I hadn't looked around outside, and I didn't do it then either. I confidently continued, slowly pressing my body up against his as I spoke. "I know how you feel about me. I feel that way too. I know we cannot do anything about it just yet, and perhaps never... but whatever you *do* want to do that doesn't break their rules... I'm willing to do too."

I then reached up and pressed my lips against his. "There. That didn't break any rule, did it?" He shook his head and so I kissed him again, harder, my lips parting and my tongue delicately licking his upper lip as soon as his lips parted in response. His tongue then thrust into my mouth, filling it, as I wrapped my lips around it and sucked on it gratefully, caressing it with my own tongue. Our bodies pressed against each other dangerously, and I could feel an erection grow and pulse against me through his jeans as I began to moisten inside, my body preparing itself for something that was not going to happen. I broke away and looked up at him. "Break any rules yet?" I asked.

"Don't know," he responded, panting as he spoke. "We might be getting by on a technicality."

I nodded and dove in a third time. Our arms were wrapped around each other and began roving to different areas, exploring body parts that were just at the borderline of erogenous zones without actually straying too far, although coming close. *So damned close...*

We broke away as if on cue, and walked further into the room, hoping that whoever kept watch on us from outside didn't think much of the extra time it took to walk from the door to the parts of the room that were more easily visible from outside. And also hoping that they couldn't tell how ragged and strained our breathing was. I grabbed my hair with both hands and threw it back, then settled into a sitting position on my bed. Bill opted for the nearby chair instead.

After a moment or two to collect ourselves, I asked, "So how do you wanta work this?"

"If we just do this, we're likely to drive ourselves crazy," he replied. "But if that's all I can get, I'll take it." He looked me in the eye, putting the ball in my court.

"Touching isn't—" I began, unsure of how best to word my thoughts. "No one ever got impregnated by touching," I concluded.

"Or... other things," he added, haltingly. "There are plenty of things that wouldn't result in impregnation of any kind." We weren't looking at each other at this point, simply stealing shy glances as we tentatively put out these suggestions.

"But we would be easily observed," I mentioned. "There's no way to carry on in secrecy here."

Bill dropped his head and nodded. "No, you're right. Either way, this is something that has to be proposed to the alpha of the pack." He kept glancing over at the window now, and I realized that this visit would soon have to end. I stood up and he did too, obviously thinking the same thing that I was. I looked at the window and then went to the door, and when he approached I pulled him to me for a passionate kiss, one arm hooked around his neck and one leg bent and wrapped around his thigh, both doing their best to hold him as tightly to me as possible. He ravaged my mouth and began grinding his lower body against me when he suddenly stopped and pulled away, a distracted and troubled look on his face. But there was no one in sight, so I couldn't explain his reaction. I turned the knob and opened the door for him without complaint and he quickly passed by me and went outside, but not before I realized the possible reason for his behavior: premature ejaculation? He must have gone without for too long and then got too excited too quickly. My attitude change toward him, and the way I attacked him when he got through the door, and then the way we stopped suddenly and then started up again, would clearly result in such an outcome.

I gauged my own body's condition, and found that my own state of arousal was also past the reversal point. I looked around the room, then out the window, and hated the thought of being constantly under surveillance like this. I found a safe haven from prying eyes in the bathroom, and stayed in there for ten minutes before emerging in a more composed state, in order to write this latest journal entry.

EIGHT

It was two nights before I saw Bill next. I had the feeling he was avoiding me, and perhaps more than a bit embarrassed about what I believe happened to him before he left. But he was apparently over it now, and ready to discuss our next move. I told him that I didn't feel comfortable talking with Jack about it yet, and also mentioned that I was beginning to become obsessed with the moon. He told me that was natural, but I didn't think it was.

"You don't understand. I'm watching it constantly for the slightest change—and it's still only a sliver! I'm dreading every expansion on its part and agonizing over it becoming a half, because I know that not far behind that is a full moon! And when that happens..." I couldn't continue, and he took me into his protective arms, not caring if anyone saw.

"You're just waxing," he told me, as if that would take all the anxiety away. "I'm waxing too," he added, but the look of desire in his eyes proved that the term meant something different for him than for me. "I need to see you."

"We can't be too obvious about it," I cautioned. "Let's just go about our business and then save it for when we say good night, like the other day."

He nodded vigorously. "What would you like to do today?"

"Why Bill," I teased, "do you plan all your dates this way? I thought you'd have organized something a little more definite than this. A carriage ride through the park, a picnic in the field..."

"A meal and a game of pool over at the Social Center?" he offered. "I'd do better, but we're sorta limited in where we can go and what we can do. The weekend passes haven't come in yet," he added jokingly.

"Okay, sailor boy, but don't expect much then."

"Like I said before," he replied, "I'll take what I can get."

. . . . .

The days had gotten easier. Ever notice how your troubles take a back seat when you're in love? I spent my days thinking of ways to be with Bill without everyone knowing what was going on, and my nights dreaming of what we had done, and of what more I would have loved to do with him. We still followed the Golden Rule, after all. We were just... looking for loopholes and testing just how far we could bend it without breaking it. The most frustrating part was that we usually could only spend three or four minutes with each other in this fashion, for fear of attracting attention to ourselves. Wherever we could find a moment alone we took it—but no longer than that.

But once only half the moon was covered in shadow, my fear returned, and not even our sexual foreplay could ease my anxiety. I stopped meeting Bill as much, and even when we got together for meals, I went home afterward alone.

Bill's waxing was nothing like mine was, but it definitely affected him just as strongly. He was more excited, easily aroused, and constantly eager for more. And I'm not just referring to his sex drive, for I had temporarily stopped providing in that department. He was strangely expectant and always on edge, like a predator eager to pounce, upon food, upon game, upon me. He reveled in his state of excitement, clearly enjoying his canine influences and the entire change that comes upon him as the moon approaches full. He was never scary to me, and didn't come across as dangerous, but I didn't exactly appreciate the way he loved the whole process, especially considering my disdain for what was about to happen to me in just under a week.

Going to sleep at night became difficult, and I started to view the night itself as a menacing enemy, stalking in wait for me to expose myself and submit to its dark charms, which I didn't want to do. My dreams lost their erotic flavor and became filled with feral images of violence and carnage, and occasionally of bestiality, which was worst of all. I would awake in a sweat, only to find that the night had not left, but lay in wait some more, influencing my mind with dark imagery and patiently planning its conquest of my body. For physically I was still a creature of the dawn, still human in every sense I possessed. But I knew that this would change when the moon completed its cycle, and even though I had had three weeks to try to prepare myself for this eventuality, I was still fighting the inevitable with every fiber of my being. I was *human*! I would not lose that to become something else! I would resist, fight it, beat it somehow! I would not let it take me!

NINE

Two A.M. There are wolves outside, running and howling. It is their time. It is not mine. I have taken to writing whenever I wake from a night terror, to help calm myself down and keep hold of my humanity. The moon is less than half covered in shadow. I realize that I could stop it from happening if I take my own life tonight. I haven't lived through a full moon yet, haven't undergone a transformation, don't yet feel any different physically than I felt a month ago. Perhaps I could take my life and my body wouldn't regenerate because I have not become one of them yet. Perhaps I could prevent the transition to wolf by dying before the full moon. Dying a human being. Thwarting Jack's actions and taking back my mortality. By ending it.

TEN

One-thirty A.M. The moon is gibbous. I mentioned my plan to Bill today. I am a coward and cannot take my own life. I need his help. He refused and told me that it won't work. I believe he just said that to trick me into not trying, for he grew worried when I told him. I said that if he loved me he would do it. He replied that he couldn't do it *because* he loved me so much. I told him I hated him and didn't want to see him. I am alone again.

ELEVEN

Three-fifteen A.M. Feeling stupid about yesterday. How could I think about doing such a thing to myself when I didn't take into consideration another possibility. Maybe I won't change! Maybe it didn't work. Maybe Jack didn't bite hard enough, maybe his saliva didn't enter my bloodstream. Maybe *I* am somehow immune to all this. It's possible! And if so, just look at how many Dingoes could be saved! They could find out what it is about me that makes me immune and then come up with some sort of cure for the rest! And then Bill and I... could return to our own people and make a life amongst them. How selfish I was to not think of this, to not think of *them*. It's not all about me. I have to endure, have to be strong and wait it out, prove to them that I could be their savior. And to think, I almost took that hope away from them.

TWELVE

Eleven-forty-five P.M. I foolishly told Bill what I believed. He told me that all Dingoes go through that "What if it doesn't happen to me" stage and think that they might be special and unique right before the first full moon. And then they all end up changing regardless. Nevertheless, I am holding on to this one chance. I will not give in until I am proven to be mistaken. Even if I wake up the day after the full moon with blood on my teeth and a dead rabbit hanging from my mouth, I will still not believe. This could very well be an elaborate hoax! Or some sick, twisted experiment run by the government... Maybe we were drugged into believing that the things we thought we saw are all real. There are endless possibilities. How absurd of me to accept what they told me as truth. To buy into this whole werewolf nonsense and think that I was one of them, when clearly I'm not! How clearly one thinks in the middle of the night. I should spend more of the night awake and sleep during the day as the rest of them do in this community.

THIRTEEN

Midnight. I strolled out into the night air and was not surprised at how many wolves were outside. I looked up at the moon, which was nearly full, and could not tell much of a difference between that and an actual full moon. Bill was outside too, staring up at the moon as well. He saw me and came over, and asked how I was doing.

"I know, I was a bit of a fruitcake this past week," I replied. I was no longer acting irrational, and a strange calm now possessed me. Perhaps it was acceptance — the final stage of grief — but I still believed that there was a chance that nothing was going to happen to me. Although I now acknowledged that it might.

"Typical for one's first month," Bill mentioned. "Especially as one gets closer to that first full moon."

"Please. Don't remind me." I said.

"Don't remind you? You're out here staring at the moon, which is nearly full."

"Okay, that was a stupid thing to say," I admitted.

"That's okay, I've heard you say stupider things in the past couple of days," he said with a smirk.

"Laugh it up," I said wryly to him. "Although I probably do deserve that."

He looked me in the eye. "Actually, you've had us all pretty scared with some of the things you were saying. Talking about taking your own life and all."

"I know. Don't worry. It'll all be over tomorrow. One way or the other. Either I'll have nothing to worry about because nothing happens, or I'll have nothing to worry about because I'll have slept through it as if nothing happens. Right?"

"Yep."

"It *is* tomorrow that it starts, isn't it? Not the *technical* full moon but the night before?"

"Uh-huh. Three nights of fun."

I looked up at the moon and commented on how it already looked full to me.

"No," Bill observed. "The outer edge is not visible, but by tomorrow it will be, although slightly shaded."

Loud talking caught my ear, particularly because it was just that: *talking*, and not barking or howling. We looked over to see Jack speaking with a stranger as they approached our cabins, and I was only barely conscious of the fact that anyone out in wolf form had scattered, leaving only a few of Jack's muscle around, the big burly men whom I encountered that first night.

Bill was making a point of trying not to look like he was watching the exchange, even as the group neared us, so I also deliberately looked away, while stealing the occasional sidelong glance whenever I dared. When they had retreated inside one of the larger cabins reserved for "administrative business," I turned to Bill and asked him what that was about.

"Whatta ya think? Remember what brought me into the acquaintance of these people? My story on squatters?"

"Who?"

"Squatters," he repeated. "People who settle in on property that doesn't belong to them? You might've heard the term before? Okay, so maybe it's not the glamorous type of crime they make movies about often. But it *is* still a crime, and you can be sure the feds are after them, and the rest of the communities spread across these glorious states. They probably don't have a clue as to the actual nature of their quarry, but then these simpleminded government servicemen probably wouldn't even care about that. I bet if they'd captured one of these canines and learned of what they are, they'd just say, 'That's nice; now about these squatting charges you're being brought up on...'"

"So I take it that means we'll be on the move soon?" I ventured.

"I suspect so. But they'll want to hold off until after the full moon if they can so that they can move us Dingoes without difficulty." I looked at him, a sudden realization reflected in my troubled eyes. "They've got numerous stalling tactics they can try, to postpone federal action as much as possible. Remember, they've got years of experience doing it. I don't think we have to worry." His words were meant to reassure me, but I could tell that he was also trying to convince himself, and I don't think he was a hundred percent successful at it.

As if I didn't have enough to fret over, now there was the very real and possible threat of being euthanized on top of it all. If only Jack could stave off the feds for three more nights.

I turned to Bill and told him that I wanted to turn in for the night, and he could see and hear how despondent I had become and offered to walk me back. As I slid inside the doorway, I remained in his path and turned to him, blocking the entrance from behind the door.

He noticed that the door was between us and asked if I wanted him to come in for a minute, panting slightly as he asked. I would have thought that my posture would have made my intention clear, but I answered anyway that I wasn't in the mood tonight. He remained with his head leaning forward, just inside the doorway, panting a bit heavier as he fought to think of something that might persuade me to change my mind, and then he straightened up and cleared his throat, and bid me a quiet goodnight.

I don't know why I didn't let him in; it might have been just what I needed to get my mind off the many troubling thoughts invading my mind. But quite honestly, I wasn't in the mood for any erotic encounter; it just didn't feel appropriate with all that was going on. With regard to Bill, I didn't want to cause him any additional suffering, and felt bad for rejecting him, but there was nothing I could do about that. He should understand; he's been very understanding about everything so far. Inside, I dropped onto the bed and thought about full moons, transformations, feds, werewolves, euthanasia, and Bill. And somehow I did manage to fall asleep.

FOURTEEN

I awoke to the last day of my life as a mortal, for until my first transformation I could still think of myself as human, but afterward I would forever consider myself a monster. I dressed quickly and headed out early to find Bill. I hoped he was not too upset about being rejected the night before, and wanted to make sure everything between us was still the same. I went to the Social Center, but he was not there. After a fast omelet and coffee I went out in search of him again, following a lead from Cookie that he might be found at the school, even though classes were cancelled during the first few days leading up to a full moon due to the agitated state of the Dingo teachers in their waxing (which in this case applied to just me and Bill).

Sure enough, there he was with Jez, finishing up some school-related discussion. I waited until they were done talking and then stepped into pace beside him as he headed back the way I had just come. He seemed restless and slightly anxious, and so I asked him if he were okay. He looked at me with a haggard expression, his wild eyes contrasting a thoroughly exhausted face. He seemed at a loss for words, which was very unlike Bill, and muttered something about waxing and needing to be alone. I was put off by this uncharacteristic behavior (after all, he did say that he didn't experience such a waxing state), and I stopped in my tracks, letting him continue on by himself.

I suddenly sensed Jez at my side, and was embarrassed by the sympathetic look she gave me. Then I panicked, fearing that she could see what was really between Bill and me.

"Don't worry honey; it's just the waxin'. He'll act friendly to you once again once this full moon stage is passed. Ask Cookie. He avoids her and every other female Dingo in the community during this time of month. Prob'ly the best thing too; he knows himself best. If you thought a man's drives are strong under normal conditions, just imagine how they are when his senses are heightened to the point of no control. I'll bet he wishes it was night already, so he can change and vent some of his passions and desires in the night."

"While he's asleep," I added.

Jez turned from the sight of Bill's retreating form and looked me full on. "That boy don't sleep. He may not be himself, and he may not remember any of what happens during his time as a wolf, but his urges are so powerful the drugs don't last long on him and he's up howlin' and tearin' at his chains and makin' a damn nuisance of himself month after month after month. Now don't get me wrong, I think he's wonderful, great with the pups, a fitting mate for any lucky woman..." I shot a worried look her way, but she was once again looking after her colleague's diminishing shape, only half-looking in my direction. "But just like a dog that's been pent up for too long in a small apartment, he needs a good run under the stars every once in a while, and it's a shame he can't do it. It's been tried with some Dingoes that resist the drugs and seem to need to get out, but often it leads to them getting away from us and out into society, causing another werewolf story and a messy clean-up job for our spin-doctors. Not to mention continued damage to our already tarnished reputation as a species."

She put a hand on my shoulder and then let it trail off as she moved away, back toward her school. Before entering, she turned to me and added mischievously, "Oh, by the way, if you two are *really* careful..." Needless to say, she had my full attention as I stood there frozen in place, suspicious of what she was about to say and hoping no one else could hear. "Teacher's lounge, behind my office, no windows." And then she was gone. And I still remained frozen in place, feeling naked and afraid, not daring to even turn my head and see if there were any witnesses to overhear her message to me.

I was on my way back to the Social Center when I was

approached by fellow Dingo Samantha, who popped out of the nearby woods so suddenly that I was worried that she might have been listening in and waiting for the right moment to approach me. But if this were true, she certainly didn't show it on her face, and I concluded that if she were waiting for me, she was too wrapped up with delivering her message to me properly that she didn't bother to concern herself with my business with Jezebel.

"Bev—is it okay that I called you Bev?—I was sent here by Jack—you know, our pack leader—to fetch you to his room—Don't worry you're not in trouble or anything—at least as far as I can tell—but what do I know really—Anyway, it's this way."

Her message, delivered in her usual—or unusual—rapidfire manner, left my head spinning, but I dutifully followed her to a meeting with our alpha, the purpose behind which I couldn't begin to fathom, but for some reason left me feeling very uncomfortable. But I guess I should be grateful that it was Samantha, and not Aryana, that came to get me. I hoped that this reflected the level of importance the meeting would have. Would they really send their "omega" for me if this was urgent or something I should worry about? Besides, Jack had been pretty decent to me after the Ricky incident, and I found that my dislike of him was not as severe as it had been. Of course, I can't say the same for Aryana.

· · · · ·

Samantha opened Jack's door without knocking, and then surprised me by entering ahead of me instead of departing upon carrying out her orders. Inside Jack was sprawled half-naked on a king-sized bed, and my misgivings returned to me in full force as I saw Samantha literally curl up into a ball at his feet, while two *Canis sapien* females in human form bedecked the alpha leader, kissing and licking him on the face, neck, and chest, and applying tender ministrations that he did not even take notice of. I wanted to bolt from the room.

But true to my spirit, I wasn't about to let him see my discomfort, and I strode up to the bed as if this were a proper meeting, in a business office with perhaps a secretary or two attending. I tried to hold onto that image so that my artificial composure wouldn't break, and I believe I pulled it off beautifully for at least a full minute. It would have been worse if Aryana had also been present. Thinking about the alpha's bitch actually helped, as it allowed me the option of expressing outrage, even though I already understood the peculiar relationship between an alpha and his bitch, and between an alpha and all the females in his pack.

He watched me through eyes half-shut, prolonging my agony by maintaining a silence that was broken only by the soft, languid gestures of his females. I was finding it hard to keep it together, and before I was forced to collapse weeping from the strain I blurted out "You wanted to see me?"

"Mmm," he murmured, but whether it was in response to me or to his attendants' actions I was not sure. Then he sat forward and addressed me a bit more properly, except that what little he was wearing seemed to fall off more, exposing his well-toned, nicely haired body. "Beverly. Let's be bluntly honest. You're a desirable woman."

Oh God, it's what I feared.

"The sight of your body lights fires inside any red-blooded man."

And could he use a more corny come-on line?

"Personally I don't know what the appeal is, but then my tastes tend to the more canine."

Huh?

"For the next few days perhaps it would be best if you kept your distance from anyone... not able to suppress their shapeshifting abilities."

Ohhh. That's what this was about.

"Do you know," he continued, "that during the daylight hours of a full moon—which is visible during the day if you hadn't realized—

our Dingo hookers are put to work the most, in order to sap some of the drive out of their customers, and satisfy some of their primal lusts that are at their peak during this time of month?"

I looked at Samantha, who was gazing at me and nodding affirmation, but what I couldn't get past was the fact that the full moon would be out during the day, not just at night, and it would be affecting us during our waking hours. I hadn't realized that until now.

"You too will have primal lusts," he directed at me. "You too will have to decide how to handle them. I understand this concept of *bestiality* that disturbs you so, but in my understanding of this expression's definition, bestiality is having carnal knowledge with a mindless beast, an average animal, which *Canis sapiens* can hardly be compared to. An average beast wouldn't show tenderness during the act. An ordinary animal wouldn't treat it like an act of love." He stood on the bed, and any shreds of clothing fell from him, leaving me to see his naked human form in all its perfection. "I think you have a misconception about what sex with one of us could be like. That is why you are here." Samantha repositioned herself so that she was on her elbows and knees, facing me at the foot of the bed. Her back was slightly flattened toward the bed, leaving her rump lifted in the air behind her. She was wearing a pleasant, loose dress, similar to many worn in Jez's house of pleasure, and the two females on either side of the bed flipped it up so that her body was exposed beyond her shoulder blades. Her backside was petite and firm, and in its current position it made the shape of a heart.

A slight shimmer above her caught my attention, and I looked up just in time to see Jack transform into the shape of a wolf behind her. *Directly* behind her, between her legs to be precise! I was scandalized by the sight, but I couldn't turn from it, due either to shock or curiosity I know not which and was afraid to conjecture. His front paws on her back, they clawed at her without exposed nails, leaving her skin unpierced and simply caressed. In fact Samantha began to move gently to the smooth touch of his furred limbs against her soft flesh. She closed her eyes briefly, revelling in the sensation, and then returned her gaze to me, her smile speaking volumes about the forbidden pleasures I was unwillingly witness to.

At the first thrust, my hand flew to my mouth, which had opened wide along with my eyes, betraying my absolute disgust. Samantha's head was tilting back sharply, and behind and above I could see Jack's wolf head also pointing up, as if he were about to start baying at the ceiling. The two females remained in human form but sunk back to the head of the bed, out of the way and almost out of sight. It did please me to note, however, that I was not in the least turned on by any of what I saw. In fact, I found that I could watch no more of it, and turned on my heel and bolted out the door. I slammed the door shut and put my back against it, leaning on it for support, or perhaps to shut in Pandora's evils with my puny strength. I had felt myself on the verge of regurgitating my small breakfast, but fortunately the fresh air stripped me of that unpleasant urge. And speaking of unpleasant urges, I could hear the moans and groans, both human and canine, that emanated from within the cabin I had just exited, and I pushed myself off the door that had held my weight and dashed away from the lodge with no definite heading in mind.

It didn't take long for me to catch a glimpse of that cursed moon in the sky, quite sharp and bright as it hung in the air ready to torment all the lost souls like myself on the world below it. How is it that I had never noticed its presence during the day before? How could I miss such a pronounced thing in the sky? It's for certain that I will never miss it again.

I stood still and stared up at it, gauging myself for any physical reaction I might feel under its presence, but the only reactions I had were all mental and emotional, and were concerned with events that were certain to transpire once darkness falls. But these feelings were not being transmitted to me by the moon; I was producing them myself, and I would be feeling them no matter where I was at the moment.

I looked up again and for a fleeting moment I could see the beauty and splendor of that magnificent satellite that has caused so many great scholars and poets and writers and scientists to dream of doing what had once been an impossibility: to leave the earth and touch the moon! Say what you will about our nearest celestial neighbor, but it probably did inspire more great minds to accomplish wondrous achievements than any other single entity, with the exception of the fear of death, which admittedly has also sparked milestones in our evolution.

Looking at the craters and features that even during the day seemed quite pronounced, I actually found it to have a calming effect on me, as if it were telling me not to worry about tonight, that it would be there to hold my hand through the worst of it. And I understood why its features were given such names as Sea of Tranquility.

But wait—what if these feelings were not my own? What if this was part of the moon's effect on Dingoes? Could I be so easily influenced, simply by staring up at it under the full light of day? My God, if that were so, what was tonight going to be like?

I turned from the sphere to head somewhere where I could avoid it, anywhere indoors. It was either the Social Center, or my own room. Did I want to be alone, or surrounded by people? Actually I didn't want to be by myself just then, but I didn't want to be around so many people either. Just one would have been preferable. One in particular. Bill.

There was so much that I wanted to talk to him about, so much that I had to tell him, such as my incident with Jack and with the moon. But I didn't want to make his waxing any more difficult than it apparently already was, and it was quite obvious that my presence would do just that. So I went back to the school grounds, where I could be with the one other person I felt comfortable with, Jezebel.

· · · · ·

Jezebel was a help. She got me through the day with accounts of other Dingoes' experiences during the full moon, although I suspect she was specifically selecting stories where the subjects had an unusually easy time of it. But I was grateful. The last thing I needed to hear just then was a bunch of horror stories. I returned to my room with an optimistic sense of hope that my trials will be more like those in Jez's tales.

A few hours later Aryana appeared at my door. She explained that Jack was occupied with pressing matters and that she would be the one to tie me down for the night. I was naturally distressed by this, but considering the encounter I had just had with Jack, perhaps it was for the best.

She certainly wasn't as gentle or understanding about it. After ordering me to down a flask of water in order to encourage urination, she put me in chains naked without even a scarf or kerchief to protect the tender flesh on my wrists, a courtesy Jack had provided the month before that I had assumed to be standard procedure but was in fact an uncharacteristic nicety on his part. At least the blanket to lie on was standard procedure!

She then gave me another flask, this time with a murky red fluid inside that smelled like wine. "This is the one to make you sleep," she informed me. "Don't drink too fast or too much, or else I'll have to let you go to the bathroom again." She checked her watch. "And I do have other rounds to make, including my own responsibility..." (meaning Bill). "I've made it pretty strong, so sip it just enough till you feel its effects, and when you're starting to feel drowsy put it down."

Well, here it is. The moment I've dreaded for an entire month. I drank slowly as directed, but I did drink deeply, hoping to get the full effect of the drug to knock me out completely. I wanted to be one hundred percent asleep for the transformation, and I also hoped to be so drugged that my wolf form stayed asleep and didn't thrash around and do damage to anything, including myself.

I looked up at Aryana looking down at me, and as she reached out a hand for the flask I held I recall not wanting to give it to her. Her hands were on her hips and she gave me that superior look she does so well. I was slumping against the wall from my kneeling position and considered lying down on the blanket.

. . . . .

I opened my eyes. When did they close? Where was Aryana? It took another minute to realize that the sun was shining in on me. Was it morning? I sat up. I looked down at my bare body and saw no evidence of anything different. I was still myself, regardless of what I may have been a few hours ago. And I realized that that was what was disturbing me the most, the fear that after my first transformation I would no longer be me, no longer feel like myself.

Was that it? If so, it was nothing!

But maybe it *was* nothing. Maybe nothing had happened to me in the night. How could I know?

I know, all Dingoes supposedly went through this, thinking that they were different or special and that it might not happen to them. But how was I to know otherwise? The only telltale sign that I had been through anything last night was the skin on my wrists, which were bruised and sore from the harsh metal of the chain cuffs.

"Beverly?" came a voice at the door.

"Bill?" I answered uncertainly. Wasn't he trying to avoid me?

Before I knew it he had opened the door, to both our embarrassment. I struggled to gather the blanket about my nude figure, while he struggled to avert his eyes from said figure, and was apparently having the tougher task of the two.

"I-I. . ." he stammered, blushing and finally looking away. "I'm sorry, I thought they had come for you already. I wanted to see how your first night was." He was still in the doorway, and a second later Aryana brushed past him, eyeing him severely. She addressed him as she explained.

"I checked on her before and gave her the wake-up potion, but she was still too heavily asleep to wake up. I told you not to drink so deeply last night," she added with a glance in my direction. Back to Bill she instructed, "Leave me with her and I will have her dressed and ready in no time. You can catch up with her at the Social Center, where I'm sure she will want to go at once for breakfast."

She was right. I was starving. But whether it was because of some unsatisfied hunger I experienced in the night or whether it was a natural side effect of the drug, I didn't know. I still clung to the hope that nothing *had* happened to me in the night, and until I saw proof otherwise I would not think differently.

Aryana was closing the door after Bill and heading in my direction with the key to my bonds. "How was it?" she inquired as she unlatched the cuffs. The raw bruises on my wrists were now exposed in all their glory, surprising even me as to the extent of the injuries. Maybe I had thrashed about a lot in the night? If so, that might suggest that I had indeed transformed. Of course, it was entirely possible that I simply had sensitive skin, especially considering the thin flesh of the wrists. I was uncertain, but beginning to worry. Now there was slight evidence against my belief.

· · · · ·

At the Social Center I wolfed down my food (no pun intended) with gusto. Even Bill looked at me askance as he calmly picked at his own plate. "More?" he asked when I had gobbled up everything in front of me and couldn't help but look around for more. "Cookie, a second helping," he ordered for me, perhaps fearing for the safety of his own meal. "How'd it go last night?"

"That's what I wanted to ask you about," I said, turning to him with sudden interest. "In the morning... how do you know that anything happened? I don't feel any different. As far as I can tell, nothing at all happened to me last night."

"Then the drugs did their job," he responded simply. "Most of the girls here have the same experience as you."

And then nothing. I had expected him to go on, as he usually does, but he ended there, without mentioning his own experience. I couldn't let it go at that, however, and prompted him to continue.

"Okay, you're one of the lucky majority," he explained. "The drug doesn't work very well on me; I wake up later on right before changing."

"Right *before*... or...?"

"During, yes. I get a brief feeling of what it's like to be one of them. I feel the moon's pull, experience the hunger, the drive, the desire to run out in the wild. I even feel the horrible despair of what it's like when such an animal with such strong urges finds itself confined, shackled, unable to move beyond thrashing about in its chains." He paused, but I didn't need to push him to go on this time. "And then it's morning and I slowly calm down from it all." He turned to me with a smile that was meant to cheer himself up more than me. "And here you see me." He turned back to picking at his food, but I could see that his heart was still not in it.

Then a thought struck me. "But you're the one always raving about their lifestyle. I would think you'd hate it more than me."

"No. It's because I get a taste of what it's like to be them that I relish it so much."

Cookie dropped more food in front of me, and gave me a crooked smile. "I thought you'd be wanting more, so I made extra just in case. Let me know if you want thirds."

"Cookie, how was *your* night last night?" I asked eagerly before she could leave, hoping that my keeping up this topic wasn't being insensitive to Bill.

"You know me, darlin', slept like a babe," she replied cheerily, but for some reason the reply, along with the overly pleasant attitude, seemed to me to be a practiced affectation. I didn't buy it. But I wasn't going to pry. With Bill it was different; I was closer to him than... Actually I have become closer to him than any non-relative I could think of.

"Thanks," I said, turning to the food she offered me. "Ow," I yelped softly as I repositioned myself over my plate. I rubbed my wrists gently and Bill noticed my bruises for the first time.

"Where did you get those?" he asked in genuine surprise, though I thought it would have been obvious.

"From the chains. Aryana forgot to slip a scarf between my skin and the metal." I held them up to him. "Lovely, huh?"

"A scarf?" Bill repeated, perplexed.

"Yeah, Jack provided one last month," I replied simply between forking in mouthfuls of grub. Then I looked up and noticed the confusion on his face.

He noticed me studying him and then smiled and said, "Probably a girl thing. They don't give me anything like that. It'd be pointless anyway for me." And he chuckled unconvincingly.

He again eyed me as I attacked my food. "You seem to be in better spirits than you have been lately," he observed.

"I am, I—I feel so relieved. I had been dreading last night for an *entire* month, and now that it's over I could just..." I lifted my hands in the air and didn't know what I 'could just' do. Scream? Shout for joy? Do a dance?

"You feel alive. And you'll feel this way for the next two days.

Then the waning will begin." He was smiling, but this time I could see that it was genuine, caused by his feelings for me, that I had finally gotten through the worst of it. "About this morning..." he began, but didn't know how to proceed with his explanation/apology.

"At least Aryana didn't forget my blanket," I quipped lamely.

"Yeah," he agreed, equally as lamely, but still unsure of what to say next.

"All right look. You saw me naked. We both know that. Now how can we get past that?"

"Um, I... You... There's..."

"Quite the conversationalist, Bill," I teased. "Come on, let's not spoil everything now. We've come so far in our friendship."

"Friendship?"

"Bill. Not here," I warned.

"Then where? When?" He leaned forward eagerly, breathlessly.

"Bill, I thought this was a bad time for you. Yesterday you didn't want to have anything to do with me. And now—"

"Yesterday was a mistake. It only made it worse," he quickly cut in.

I looked down at my plate, but was no longer thinking of food. I didn't know what to say to him. I didn't want to do anything that would make him worse, but now he was proposing that being together might make things *easier* for him. That went against what everyone else was telling me. Who knew better? Bill, who was going through it himself? Or the *Canis sapiens*, the supposed experts who have witnessed this behavior in countless Dingoes throughout the ages? But who didn't experience it firsthand...

"Okay," I whispered. "Later on. In the afternoon. I have a place we could go to be alone." He looked at me, both surprised and impressed. Now to change the subject, or else that's all we were going to be talking about all day: "So how is it during the winter? I mean, all we're given is a blanket that we'll most likely throw off in the middle of the night?"

"They provide heating, don't worry. The blanket's not meant for warmth but for something soft to lie on instead of a hard floor." Good, we're on to another topic. Or so I thought. "Look, if you want to even the score, you can see me naked," he added with a nervous laugh. "Oh! I've got something to show you!"

"Already?" I asked weakly. Before this the thought of Bill's body unclothed fueled my fantasies and my dreams, but now I was too concerned about where this would lead and the effects it would have on him in the night, under the full moon.

"No, not that," he said, embarrassed. "It has nothing to do with us." That was good. "Well, not directly," he added uncertainly.

He piqued my curiosity, that's for sure. Then he rose to leave and told me to meet him in a half hour at the school. The school! Was his secret the same as mine? But he did say that it really didn't have to do with us, so it couldn't be that. Could it?

· · · · ·

Outside the Social Center I strolled slowly, enjoying the outdoor air. An effect of my currently suppressed feral nature? I tried not to think about its cause and just reveled in the wondrous feeling. I came across a wolf or two on my way, but for some reason they did not concern me. I didn't think anything of it, walking among such animals. I guess that was because I was now officially one of them.

And then I came across *him*, that gray one with the white on his head, the one that acted so self-consciously when I first encountered him. He was off to the side, acting like he didn't even see me, but somehow I could tell that it was just that, an act. He was intentionally trying to look like he wasn't checking up on me, but I just knew that was what he was doing. But why? Who was this strange-acting wolf?

And what was his connection to me?

He wasn't one of my guards. After all the time I've been here, I was able to spot them with their dogs, and was even able to tell them apart from the rest of the canines. In fact, I even knew what they looked like in human form. And they didn't keep such close vigil on me anyway, simply keeping a distant observation on me to make sure I didn't go where I was not allowed to go, or that I didn't spend too much time alone with a certain male Dingo.

He—She?—I hadn't checked, but I always had the impression that it was a "he." He casually looked my way, blinked, and then moved on nonchalantly. I had seen him a few times during the month, not that many, nowhere near as often as all the others which I have come to know to a small degree. But I have to say that this was his best performance yet. If I hadn't already caught him before acting nervous around me and if this was my first time meeting him, I wouldn't have thought anything of it. But knowing of his strange behavior when near me, and also the simple fact that he was never around during public events and gatherings, I always watched him with a keen eye, to see what he was up to.

Maybe he wasn't part of this pack. Maybe he was a visiting dignitary like a Hyena, except that for some reason (advanced age perhaps?) he was lingering around longer than normal in this community. I would have to finally ask Jack about him once and for all.

When the time came to meet Bill I had major trepidation. What was he going to show me, this thing that didn't have anything to do with us directly, but maybe slightly? Or was it what I suspected, that he found the room Jez had told me about, the one with no windows, and wanted to try it out? But as I approached him, he glanced both ways and then led me *away* from the school, in the direction of the bordering woods. What was he going to show me? Did he have escape in mind?

I looked around in a panic and, unsure of whether to follow him or not, I too entered the forested region that separated our community from the outside world. "The guard dogs," I breathed expectantly.

"We're not going out far enough to concern them," he responded. "Right about... here." And he stopped just short of a little clearing, not very wide but definitely man-made — or canine-made.

"What—" I began, but he hushed me with a sharp "Shh." I looked around, and then began again at a greatly reduced volume: "What are we doing here?"

"Is someone up there?" came a deep voice sounding from somewhere far off. It wasn't far off after all, I realized, as Bill pointed out the covered hole that I would not have noticed otherwise.

"There's a pit, more like a well, under that camouflage. I don't know how deep, because I haven't approached it or even entered the clearing," Bill whispered to me from the other side of the tree we hid behind.

"Is that someone from the pack who's being punished?" I ventured, although deep down I knew that wasn't the case.

"It's the federal agent we saw the other night, before the full moon," he informed me, a sense of urgency in his tone. "They put him down there yesterday. I saw it all when I left you."

Now I was outraged, as I knew Bill was too. How could they do this to one of my kind? How dare they! "What do we do?" I asked Bill, still keeping my voice low.

"We can't do anything until the full moon ends. Then we have to find a way to get word out to the outside world. I doubt we can escape, but if we could get to a phone. They only have one working one here in the community, but working together I'm sure one of us can cause a distraction while the other..." The snap of a twig caused us to freeze and slowly seek out its source. "Let's split up and sneak back to the school. We'll talk more freely there. Jez is over at her brothel."

So we separated and did our best to move soundlessly through the foliage. As for me, I found that I hardly took more than a few breaths the whole trip back, so when we were again among familiar surroundings my head was swimming slightly from lack of fresh oxygen. Inside Jez's office, we sat and planned. "Why can't we act now?" I asked.

"What if the feds raided this place and freed us? At night, without the canines to protect us, we'd run loose among our own people, slaughtering them and creating more just like us. We'd need time to prepare them for that, to make them believe us enough to take precautions and not just mow us down with their bullets. Oh, we may not die, but we'll be hurting so bad we'll wish we were dead." He had a point. "No, we need to wait until the full moon's over before we act." He was pacing by the window, casting an occasional glance outside. "Our watchers are making sure we're back outa the woods. They seem unconcerned now; I think we can relax. They'll probably stay back among the trees, so we shouldn't have to worry about being overheard."

"Bill." Perhaps it was the prospect of returning to life among our own kind, but since we were already in the right location, I decided not to wait until later. He was looking at me, waiting for me to say something, wondering why I spoke his name. But before I lay my surprise on him, I had to know one thing. "So whose side are you on now? You were always a big advocate of their way of life. All month I've heard about how you admire their society, their rules, their powers. What's changed?"

"I don't know. Maybe you're rubbing off on me, forcing my old journalistic instincts and integrity to resurface. But as much as I embrace this way of life, I won't stand by and watch them torture an innocent man who is just doing his job, and who is in the right besides."

Just what I wanted to hear. "Follow me," I said coyly, and a bit mysteriously.

Behind Jez's office was the teacher's lounge she told me about. Bill stepped in, non-understanding my behavior. "The lounge," he said simply. "So what's so special about in here?"

I closed the door behind us and pressed my back against it, turning the lock on the knob. I looked him in the eye and waved a hand about, informing him: "No windows."

He took a minute to realize where I was going with this, and then a wicked look overcame him and he rushed to me, kissing me passionately and moving his hands all over my body. I responded in turn, occasionally emitting a word or two here and there: "Can't... go all... the way... ya know. Must... not... complete... act."

"Right," came his own monosyllabic reply. Then his mouth spoke no more and planted itself on my blouse over my nipple, pressing it between his lips through the fabric that did nothing to inhibit the sensation I was feeling.

"Oh!" burst through my own lips, making me suddenly aware of our watchers outside. But then Bill's mouth covered my own and I was able to moan all I wanted to into his own, panting, slobbering mouth.

He backed away, and with a sly smile said, "Time to even the score." And with that he unzipped his jeans and let them drop. Dingo men, however, *do* wear underwear, and in an instant those were down as well. "Now we're even."

He looked deeply into my eyes, and I could see what he wanted me to do. But I hesitated there against the door, and so he figured that my participation might be contingent on some ministrations of his own, so he grabbed my skirt and lifted it (discovering that I had eventually taken to the idea of *not* wearing underwear myself), then dropped to his knees in front of me. Obviously he felt that I would reciprocate afterward, but I still wasn't sure it should go this far. I tugged him back up to my face, and so he pressed against me instead, his naked flesh against my own. Long have I wondered what this would feel like, but not under these conditions.

He was throbbing hard, and pressing fiercely against the softness of my belly. I realized that I hadn't thought this thing through and told him "I don't know what we should and shouldn't do."

"It's just like riding a bike," he replied, grabbing the cheeks of my backside and lifting me bodily from the floor. My legs were spread on either side of him, and my vagina was poised directly over his erect member, giving me fleeting images of how criminals were impaled in the old days. He lowered me slowly, repositioning himself as necessary, and I could feel the head begin to push through my labia. I suddenly sobbed uncontrollably, and he froze and looked up at me.

I wasn't experiencing the anguish of a rape victim, since I wanted it badly, and wanted *him* even more. I was just deathly afraid of getting pregnant by him and giving birth to a poor infant who would go through exactly what we do. I don't know if there's a certain age where the transformations begin, but in my mind I saw visions of an infant strapped down by *Canis sapiens* as it changes under the full moon into a ravenous wolf pup. "NO!"

Bill lowered me to the floor, and moved back an inch. His body was convulsing from his desire to scoop me up again and proceed, but there was a pain in his expression that showed he feared that he had wronged me somehow. I was still crying too much to explain the way I felt, but before I could still my sobs and speak he was pulling up his clothes and rushing from the lounge.

I fell back against the door he had passed through and slid down it till I was slumped on the floor. I collected myself as best I could and did not attempt standing for another full minute. When I did, I stepped outside doing my best to look as if nothing had happened. My guards seemed unconcerned and remained within the woods, and I took steps in a general direction toward the heart of the community, though I knew not where I should go. I wanted to speak with Bill and tell him how I felt, but I knew that he would need a little time to calm down and recover himself, so I considered my options. I also wanted to confront Jack badly about his hostage, but at present I was not up to the challenge. The Social Center might be too crowded for me, as always, so somehow I found myself entering Jezebel's cathouse. I didn't know why I was doing it; ever since that first experience there I never set foot in the place again, but the girls I got to know to a small degree outside their place of business. For some reason, I wanted their company, which I had never really sought out before.

To my surprise I was treated like a favorite relative who's seldom seen. They doted on me and raised my spirits, and I grew to like and appreciate them like I never had before, even Samantha, who when among the other girls was not as high-strung or verbose. I enjoyed my time with them, and didn't realize how much time had passed in their company. Before taking my leave of them, I discussed with each one their feelings about the full moon and how they felt about it. It was comforting to hear that they had gone through similar experiences as me, but the bruises on my wrists were a big surprise to them. According to each one, any sores they may get from the metal cuffs disappear before they've even finished breakfast.

So when I left, I knew exactly where I wanted to go and what I wanted to do. After a stop at the Social Center, where I ordered something that required cutting with a knife, I retreated to my cabin—with the knife I had secretly pocketed—and closed the door, wishing they didn't remove the interior locks from the Dingoes' apartments.

I placed my left arm down on my little eating table and spread my pinkie as far as I could from the rest of my hand. With the stolen knife in my right hand, I placed the blade just above the left pinkie's knuckle and held it firmly in place. I then decided how best to make the slice. It was going to hurt—that much was certain—but if I really was one of them it would heal itself and begin the process of regeneration. Hopefully that would dull or even numb the pain completely.

I looked at the bruises on my wrists. The bruises that shouldn't be there. I could still feel the rawness of the flesh. A feeling that I shouldn't be having. This simple experiment would prove for once and for all whether I was an average Dingo with delusions of grandeur or whether I *was* in fact special, immune, an answer to their prayers. I pressed the blade down slightly... and must admit that the little bit of discomfort it was causing me was already scaring me off. I couldn't do it. But I needed to know; I *had* to have my answer! I repositioned and steadied the blade again. This time I moved it vertically to begin cutting, and after producing a drop of blood from an incision resembling a paper cut, I stopped again, trembling and unable to continue.

This was ridiculous! Why couldn't I do it? I looked around for something smaller than my little finger, something that might hurt less, and all I could come up with was an earlobe. But I couldn't see my earlobe to watch the processes that follow, and for me *seeing* would be *believing*. My small toe might be easier to cut off, but I'm sure it would make walking very painful for a few days. Not to mention difficult to explain. I might be able to hide my hand or ear from sight, but a limp would be too obvious, too condemning.

I held the knife before my face and studied it. It was sharp for a dinner knife but hardly a precision instrument. I put it down on the table and realized that I would not go through with it. I didn't have it in me. I slipped it back in my pocket and discreetly returned it to the Social Center, then headed over to Bill's before it got too late. Before I approached his door, it suddenly opened and Aryana stormed out, obviously enraged. She stopped short upon seeing me, and I could hear a snarl form in the back of her throat. But before I could even begin to fear what she might do to me, she moved off in a huff, stalking away at an awkward pace. Obviously being on two legs didn't suit her mood, for she was in wolf form in no time, disregarding the precautions they were supposed to take. It was okay to move about in either wolf form or human form during the daylight, but transforming in public was discouraged, especially at times when they suspected they might be under surveillance. And ever since that government official entered the campgrounds, the whole community had been on "orange alert."

I watched her and waited at the door, expecting Bill to emerge right after her and unsure what mood he'd be in. I began hearing sounds that concerned me. They were very soft; I had to strain to hear them. And they suggested to me that Bill was hurt. What had Aryana done to him? Did she know about *us*? Did she punish him somehow?

I opened the door slowly. Maybe he wasn't alone in there? Perhaps he was still being tortured inside. Maybe this wasn't about him and me but about his discovery of the pit where the federal agent was buried. I peered inside and saw Bill leaning on his bed, facing away from me. He was gasping slightly and seemed to swoon. But as far as I could tell, there was no one else in the room with him. So what had she done to him?

I was about to enter and call his name when I realized what was going on. His right arm was in front of him and moving purposefully, and the soft sounds he was making I could now identify as those of pleasure. He jerked forward, and then leaned back against the bed, turning enough to confirm my suspicions. I backed up and gently closed the door, then I high-tailed it out of there and made for my own accommodations. I wasn't the one caught in the act, and he didn't know I had seen him, but for some reason I was embarrassed more than I could ever recall being—even more than that morning when he walked in on me naked—and I was sure my face was bright red.

I had barely run more than a hundred yards when I found myself crashing into Jack. But he ignored the state I was in and simply asked if I knew what was bothering Aryana.

His question took me off guard, and I answered in as vicious a manner as I could muster. "Perhaps she saw you with your harem yesterday."

"What? Are you nuts?" he exclaimed, grabbing me by the arm. "First of all, my choice as to who is the alpha bitch depends on who I think is perfect for the position, not on any of your primitive notions of love and codependency. And *testing* other females for the position is just one of my duties as pack alpha, not to mention seeding as many as I can to pass on the traits that make me eligible for the position."

"Oh, please," I muttered, breaking out of his grip and storming off. "Typical male response. Give a man an excuse to cheat that he can justify with some half-ass rationale, and he'll proclaim that it's his God-given responsibility to fornicate with the whole world." I don't know how much of my mumbling he heard, for I had walked away without turning back, muttering more for my own sake than for his, but when I remembered that I had wanted to speak to him about the man down the hole, I turned on my heel to confront him—and he was gone.

I walked back the way I had come, to see if I could catch sight of him, but when I was back in view of Bill's cabin the only person I saw was Bill, hesitantly emerging from his room. I self-consciously averted my eyes, looking about for any sign of Jack, but when I glanced back in Bill's direction he waved to get my attention and call me over. I despondently shuffled over to him, and when I was in front of him he asked me if I saw Aryana a moment ago, leaving his room.

I had no reason to think that he suspected my presence earlier, and so I lied to him and told him that I had not seen her. "Why?" I added, hoping to learn the reason for her unusual behavior before.

"Well... I," he began with great difficulty. "She came over to... uh... see to my needs. Remember, the canine responsible for turning you into a Dingo is also responsible for... making sure you're not too excited during a full moon. And so she was here to... offer her services to me... sexually."

"And?" I prompted, still not sure why she left the way she did, or look at me like she wanted to rip my throat out.

"Well... I," he again began in the same difficult manner, "turned her down."

This was a shock to me. "But why?"

At that, Bill reddened and could not meet my gaze. But that was answer enough; I knew why. And even though he was to supply me with another good reason for his rejecting her, deep down I knew it was really because he was being faithful to me.

"Um, last month, she did something I wasn't pleased about," he offered as explanation. "In the middle of... *assisting* me, she changed into a wolf right in the middle of the act. Well, not quite the middle, more like... right before the end." He looked me in the eye to get his point across. "I don't know if she was just toying with my emotions, or trying to 'put me in my place' by reminding me of what I am and what she is. Let's just say that it left a deep impression."

"I'm sorry," I said, not knowing what else to say to that. I know what an impression it would make on me. "I had a similar experience yesterday," I added, to which he shot me a look of concern, with possibly a dash of jealousy thrown in. "Oh, no, nothing like that. It's just that Jack had me summoned to his room where he showed me what it was like to make love to one of their kind."

Bill's eyes bulged. "With Samantha!" I corrected. "I stormed out of there." He seemed more relaxed at that. "But he changed into a wolf before beginning the act. And she..." I would have left it at that but he was looking at me expectantly. "She enjoyed it. She really enjoyed it," I concluded.

"That would account for her suitability in her choice of profession," he remarked dryly. "Look, about before," he said, changing the subject. "I'm sorry about—"

"No, no, no" I interrupted, placing a hand over his mouth. "I wanted it, I really did. We just didn't think it through. We had no protection, ya know? We just rushed into it. And it's entirely my fault. I set up the whole ambush on you and forgot to lay down the ground rules first. I really want to pick up where we left off. But I don't know when would be the right time."

"I agree," he said. "Let's just try to survive this full moon phase first and then discuss it further."

"And I'll bring it up to Jack like I promised," I added, realizing that we were going to need the alpha's blessing and feeling that I had enough strong arguments to enforce a change in their policy toward us. Their Golden Rule would have to be torn down. It did more harm than good. Abstinence was no longer the order of the day—hadn't been for years. If they wanted to become part of today's society, they would also have to accept the terms we humans put on such things as sex and relationships. Our "primitive notions of love and codependency" indeed!

I kissed him on the lips, right there in the open, much to his surprise, and then I left for my room to plot my course of action. I planned to be awake this night when the full moon blazes in the sky. I wanted to meet this new me that supposedly took over during those hours, if it existed at all—and I was still not convinced it did. If Bill could do it month after month, I could certainly try it one time. I wanted to *know* the wolf I would become.

FIFTEEN

It was Aryana who once again came to give me my sleeping potion, with not a word about our previous encounter and what had taken place. She looked at my wrists as she was about to cuff them for the night, and a slightly troubled expression crossed her features.

"Shouldn't be there, should they," I commented, referring to the marks on them.

She drew forth a kerchief like the one Jack had given me the month before. "Is this what Jack used when he tied you down for the night?"

"Yes," I replied, "and he didn't drug the wine, which he said would be a shame, but instead drugged the meal he had brought me."

"That was before you were conditioned to our community life," she explained. "Now you are assumed to have eaten your fill at the Center, when and as you desire, and not to eat in your room. We're not going to hold your hand and tell you when to eat."

"No, just when to sleep and when to pee," I remarked.

"Only at this time of month and for your own protection."

Before handing me the flask with the drugged wine in it, she gave me the water to make me go to the bathroom. While I was going, something happened that I began to have my suspicions about earlier. "I'm bleeding a little," I said upon emerging from the bathroom. She froze in her tracks. "I think I'm getting my period. Something else that shouldn't be happening, isn't it?"

After a moment's hesitation, she responded matter-of-factly. "Not at all. We get it once a year. This may be when you're going to be having it from now on. So then next year at this time will be your next period."

"But I just—"

"You can't count last month; you weren't one of us yet. Now the whole cycle begins, and you'll have it again in a year." She wrapped the kerchief around my wrists and then put the cuffs on me, but as she did this I could see that she was slightly confused, and it dawned on me that her explanation was as much to make sense of it herself as it was to answer me. "Drink," she ordered, handing me the flask with the sleeping potion inside. I looked in at the wine, and swilled it around a bit before taking a sip—a small sip.

"I'm going to need something," I told her.

"What, some bread and cheese to go with it," she said sarcastically.

"No, a tampon and some underwear," I answered back.

She stood up and was about to take a step backward when she thought of something and said to me, "Drink some more."

"Of course I will," I replied, as if she were crazy to imply otherwise. "You don't think I want to be awake during it all, do you. I'll probably drink too much like yesterday, just to be sure."

"Well, I didn't fill it as much, just in case you tried that again," she told me, and I knew I had her fooled. But still she didn't budge, so I put the flask to my lips and tilted it back. I didn't let any of the liquid in, of course, and when I removed the flask from my lips there was wine dripping down the sides of my mouth. If it couldn't go in my mouth, it had to go somewhere. She looked at the streaks that formed on either side of my lips. I licked up the straying drops and made an "Mmm" sound, which seemed to satisfy her. She said she'd be back in a few minutes and to drink the rest more slowly.

When she was gone I looked about for a place to dump the rest. I was already chained, so I couldn't flush it down the toilet or pour it into the sink. But fortunately I had prepared for this and had left my bag slung over a chair just within reach. I dragged the chair to me and then opened the pocketbook, already emptied of all personal effects but stuffed with rags and toilet paper for absorption. Into it I slowly dumped the contents of the flask, leaving a little at the bottom so as not to arouse suspicion. I then slung the bag over the back of the chair once again and pushed the chair so that it was now even beyond my reach.

When Aryana returned, she found me slumped down groggily with a near-empty flask in my hands. I drained the remainder of the fluid for her benefit, and she took it from me and peered inside. She then handed me both items I had requested, and then she realized that I would probably need my hands freed and grudgingly freed them. I pretended to force myself awake as I took the proffered items, and when she saw me struggle to stand she took my elbow to help steady me.

Once again she watched me as I inserted the tampon and put on the panties, and it bothered me this time just as much as the last. The panties were not my own and felt a bit snug, to which she *had* to comment. "Oh, are you too big for those? I went by my own judgment and I guess I gave you too much credit. Either that or you've been putting a few pounds on since you joined us. I'm sure you've heard how that often happens in one's first month. I could go see if they have any larger sizes if you wish, but it would probably be for nothing anyway. You'll just rip through those in the night if your transformation is rough enough. It sucks that you have your period during the full moon. And you'll probably be ruining good underwear in the process."

"Yeah, it's an awful shame," I agreed dryly as she reattached my handcuffs. "But don't trouble yourself; these'll be fine for tonight," I said, reminding myself to slur my words. "And something tells me I'll still be wearing them in the morning."

"Why would you say that?"

Not willing to let her know of my suspicions, I dropped back down to the floor and made an effort to keep my eyes open, offering her the explanation that the drug is so strong I'd probably sleep through the whole thing again. Through slitted eyes I could see that this reasoning satisfied her, and as I tried to make my breathing natural to convince her that I was asleep, she took her leave of my cabin, peering back at me from the door for a few moments before closing it behind her.

My performance wasn't entirely an act. The drug really was strong, and what little I actually swallowed was having an effect on me already. I yawned and found that if I were not careful I would be asleep for real in no time. Looking around for something to help keep me alert, I could think of nothing that would be of assistance, certainly nothing that was within my very limited reach. Nothing, that is, except pain.

Seeking an alternative to that unpleasant option, I considered making myself vomit, but I had wanted to keep it a secret that I kept myself awake, and vomiting would leave evidence to the contrary. So I extended myself as far as the chain would let me, gritted my teeth, and yanked hard against the cuffs. The fire I felt in my wrists was excruciating, and I actually saw blood begin to stain the velvety kerchief.

This helped, and I did it as infrequently as possible but whenever I felt myself starting to go under. Fortunately, my head began to clear within the next hour, and in another hour or two I was simply drowsy from the lateness of the hour, and not from any foreign influence. It was now dark out, but surely not later than nine or nine-thirty. So when was it supposed to happen? Midnight? The witching hour?

. . . . .

The sound of howling jolted me forward, and I realized that I had nodded off briefly. I looked down at my human form and then looked around for the source of the sound that woke me up. The howling had turned to growling, and there was ferocious thrashing about and the sound of running feet. A loud crash precipitated a new rush of running feet, one of which eventually made its way in my direction. After a few minutes, during which the feet circled my cabin a few times, they slowly approached my door. It opened and a dark shape peered in on me. I screamed and my indoor light suddenly came on.

"You're awake?" Jack asked, his hand still at the light switch by the door.

"Whatta you want?" I asked, out of breath from hyperventilating.

"One of the Dingoes got loose. I wanted to make sure you were alone in here."

"Why? Who was it? *Which* Dingo escaped?" I asked, getting more anxious and more insistent with each question.

He paused and just looked me in the eye for what seemed like an eternity, then he gave in and answered what I already knew: "It was Bill."

"Get me loose. Get me outta here!" I yelled at him as he was about to turn and leave. He hesitated at the door, and then I hit upon the perfect reason for turning me loose. "I can help you get him. He'll come to me. You know that. That's why you came straight here."

That swayed him. He came in and produced a key that opened my cuffs, then helped me to my feet and threw me my shoes and the dress I had discarded earlier from where it lay on the bed. As we ran out into the night, I was grateful for the underwear I had convinced Aryana to give me. One of Jack's men told us that Bill made it to the woods. I was assured that, between the wolves chasing after him and the guard dogs at the outer edge, he should be trapped in between.

"Take me to him," I told the lackey, who looked to Jack for a sign of what to do. Jack gave an almost imperceptible nod, and the man turned into a wolf and took off toward the trees. We followed, but thankfully Jack remained in human form at my side. He never strayed far, and when we entered the forest he even made sure I didn't stumble or get tangled in low-hanging branches. His only comment to me was to not get anywhere near Bill or I would be ripped to shreds.

Shortly we came upon more of Jack's men, some in wolf form, others in human form holding various implements: heavy nets, rifles, bear traps, and others that I did not recognize. Jack made them all hang back, as the two of us crept forward. I could see his nose working furiously to pick up and keep Bill's scent, and after another hundred paces he grabbed my arm and slowed down, inching us further toward some invisible track that he could apparently see as clear as day.

And then I finally saw it: Bill's wolf. I was no longer aware of Jack at my side; I was mesmerized by the magnificent beauty and horror of what I saw. Unlike the *Canis sapiens* in their natural form, this "man-wolf" was completely unnatural. Neither wolf nor man, it existed somewhere in between, where magic and madness meet. It was the size of a man, seeming to stand even taller than Bill because of the extra layer of fur draped around him. The face was Bill's and yet it was not Bill's, as if Bill had suddenly grown the features of a wolf right in the center of his face. I could see why legends sprang up about these creatures after a sighting. Who wouldn't tell of an encounter with such an animal, especially if you *lived* to tell it!

He was splendid. He was breathtaking. He was... looking right at me!

"Bill, it's me, Beverly," I said, hoping to reach the man inside. "It's BJ, Bill, your BJ."

He turned his impressive body in my direction and sniffed the air. His howl was sudden and heart-wrenching. It made me jump, and shivers continued to travel the length of my spine long afterward. He took a step in my direction, and then another and another. All the heat seemed to have drained from my body as I watched Bill's wolf approach me. It was still far enough off, but I had lost my nerve at the sight. Its teeth were visible in the moonlight, sharp and gleaming and unbelievably long.

What was I thinking? What did I think I could do, talk to it? It's a monster! A killer! They didn't pass down tales of it to tell of its majesty and wonder. They tell of how it murdered their friend, lover, parent, or child!

There I was, watching as it stalked its way toward me, every second taking more of a toll on my sanity. "Billll," I whined. "NO!" He stopped in his tracks and cocked his head to the side in a very canine gesture. He sniffed the air, and I was suddenly uncomfortable in my recollection of what had physically returned today. Last month the scent of my period had driven him mad with desire my first night in the camp. I could only imagine what it was doing to him now, just meters away from the source. Fortunately it hadn't come on full yet, the stress of the month causing a slight delay in my cycle, as I should already be finishing up by this time of month. But as far as his advanced senses could tell, I was in heat and ready for him.

He took another step toward me and I considered running away, back to the protection of Jack's men, who seemed to have blended into the scenery and disappeared from my view. But I was deathly afraid of triggering the predator's chase reflex in Bill, so I froze where I stood and tried not to move a muscle. Even Jack was gone—or rather, not gone but in hiding, in order to close in on Bill while I had him distracted. I wondered what they would use to trap him, steel nets, strong tranquilizers, the kind they use on elephants and rhinos?

But wait. Why was Jack so concerned that I not get close to Bill? What could he do to me, turn me into one of them? But I already was one of them, wasn't I? Or was I? No, that's not it; he said it would rip me to shreds. And I suppose it would do the same to the rest of them too if it got hold of any of Jack's men. It would be wolf versus wolf-thing and I wonder which would win. And then the loser would begin the long and painful process of suffering through its regeneration. And what if its body was too far gone? Was there a point where regeneration is impossible? The words "limited regeneration abilities" came back to haunt me. *I must be crazy to be out here*, I thought frantically to myself and looked around to try to locate

Jack or any of his pack.

Bill had ceased his hesitant approach and was sniffing the trees around him, obviously detecting the presence of his hunters. In a flash, he threw his head up and gave out a sound somewhere between a snarl and a howl and then lunged headlong in my direction. Before I even had time to think of what to do, a loud gunshot exploded from slightly behind and to the left of me, and the beast that was Bill came crashing to the ground at my feet. The physical changes that his body suddenly underwent left no doubt in my mind as to what they had shot him with; I had seen its effects before. They used silver on him.

I turned from the sight, not wishing to witness it again, and looked for Jack, who popped out into the open a second later. And then I saw the one who pulled the trigger. It was Aryana. I advanced on her in fury. But I had not taken more than two steps before I was struck by the expression on her face. She was damn near in tears. This floored me, and I couldn't breathe for a moment, much less continue my mad rush on her.

She looked at me, with a mix of hate and pity, and said in a guttural voice, "I told you to stay away from him." She then couldn't keep herself together and turned her back on me and walked away.

I felt Jack leading me toward a clearing with a stump that he had me sit on. Everything was happening so fast I hadn't even had time to acknowledge Bill's murder or how I felt about it. The fact that it was by silver also hadn't registered in full yet, or it would have torn me apart then and there, reminding me of my introduction to that horrible fate and its effects. As Jack had said, the degradation of Bill's body was nowhere near as spectacular as Ricky's, due to the small trace of argentum used in the projectile fired directly into him. And his body's slow disintegration was already beginning while he was unconscious and still in wolf form, somehow making it less devastating to my tortured senses.

"Look," he said to me gently. "There's a lot we have to discuss and very little time to do it."

"Why aren't I a wolf?" I finally asked. The realization seemed to come to me as an afterthought, but the implications were staggering. "If I'm immune, there may be a cure. You didn't have to kill Bill. Why did you allow—"

"All Dingoes die tonight," he said simply. "The feds are movin' in on us tonight. Our info was wrong, or perhaps they stepped up their timetable for some reason." I immediately thought of their captive in the hole and suspected this to be the reason. "Either way, we're caught unprepared for this. There's no way of moving them during the full moon. They will either be unconscious, and thus unable to transport in our wolf form, or they'll be awake and uncontrollable. They mustn't be allowed to get loose into your society either. As you already know, what will be left of them will not be enough for your people to identify. And their altered body chemistry should even hamper any DNA testing they perform. They will be effectively erased from this world. Completely."

I shrank back with fear. It only just hit me; I was going to die this night.

"No, no," he comforted, reading my thoughts. He took a moment, swallowed, and said, "You're not a Dingo."

I hadn't heard correctly. "What?"

"You've never been bitten."

"That's ridiculous! I remember you biting me. I felt—"

"My teeth were capped. No saliva got through to your bloodstream. I used the old trick of putting a chloroform-soaked handkerchief under your nose and you were out before you realized what hit you."

I stared at him in disbelief, my mouth open, looking like a fool, which was exactly what I felt like. All that suffering. All that agonizing. My thoughts of suicide! My God, what if I had gone through with it? And those murderous thoughts I had toward Aryana in the beginning that I had attributed to the change within me? That was simply human nature? How disturbing to discover that those impulses were my own, that I could have been capable of having conceived them on my own. Jack was talking again.

"You don't know how long it took to plan this whole thing. We had to find someone with 20/20 vision, no strong personal attachments—or at least who lived alone—someone with that journalistic drive and curiosity..."

"Everyone knew I was not the real deal?" I asked weakly, feeling like the town joke.

"No, actually everyone here had no idea you were unbitten."

"You said 'we.' Who else was in on it?" I asked, grateful at least that Bill was not a part of the hoax.

A man stepped into the clearing, a man I recognized immediately though I could hardly believe my eyes.

"Professor?" I asked in disbelief. "But you're dead. I saw—"

"You saw a dead wolf and dog with animal blood smeared all over the place," came the response from the middle-aged man who started this all, who first drew me in with a story I knew could not be true but had to explore further anyway. "I stayed in wolf form the whole time you were here, and I never told you my human name in case you heard it mentioned in passing by any of the pack. Most of them were not aware of the incident you witnessed at the recreational park office. And even those who were there knew very little of what was actually going on. This 'experiment,' as I mentioned a month ago, was not authorized and was performed very 'hush-hush.'"

"But you tried to scare me off many times that night," I said to Jack. "What if I didn't keep coming back?"

"Then you wouldn't be the girl for the job," he said without concern. "We needed someone determined, committed, a real hellcat. Someone who wouldn't scare off easy but who would get pissed and come back at us all the more."

"You don't know the kind of fear you just put into us with that stunt you pulled with Bill," the Professor cut in.

"Yeah, a whole month's work woulda been all shot to shit," Jack added. His sudden insensitivity infuriated me.

"Oh I'm so *sorry*," I said to him with all the sarcasm I could muster. "Yes, that whole month of terrorizing me with the threat of euthanasia, fear of turning into a ravishing beast, causing the death of a child, considering cutting off a body part or killing myself, falling in love with someone I could never be with... All that woulda been for nothin', eh? Not even a little amusement on your part? Surely you must've gotten some pleasure outa watching me squirm at all your attempts to convince me to let you mount me!"

The professor looked at Jack with some confusion, convincing me that that little bit wasn't originally part of the plan, but Jack's response succeeded where mine didn't, and my cheeks flushed red from embarrassment. "If you weren't tryin' so hard to figure a way to get into Bill's pants, I wouldn't have had to try to seduce you away. You couldn't let the Golden Rule alone, could you? You had to get hot for one of the only two male Dingoes in the community! Why do you think Aryana's been acting the way she has lately? Sure she was a bitch to you right from the start. But towards the end she knew you would cause this to happen to him. She tried to warn you away..." He paused and collected himself before proceeding. "We're not the heartless beasts you may think we are. In fact, the whole point of this month-long experiment was to show you firsthand what kind of beings we are, so that you could go back and tell the world that we are *not* monsters, and that we're ready to join your society if you'll be open-minded and have us."

"The very existence of our race may depend on it," the Professor cut in.

"If your government wasn't about to bear down on us with everything it's got tonight, maybe we could've shown you more, convinced you better," Jack resumed. "Maybe we went too far with some of our charades, like faking the Professor's murder." I looked over at that dear sweet man who had amazingly won me over in so short a time.

"The name's Richard," he said with a smile. Yes, I thought, if only he had been the one to guide me through this month's pretenses. Then, perhaps, I wouldn't have been so angry at them.

"Anyway, it's too late now," Jack concluded. "I have some unpleasant business to take care of. Damn your kind for movin' in on us during a full moon! But don't worry, none of them will suffer. We use a combination of argentum and a stronger dose of that drug that put you to sleep. They're knocked out anyway; Bill was the only one up and about. So it will all be done in their sleep." He didn't sound at all cheered by this fact himself, and I realized how much it pained him to do what he felt he had to do next. "If it's any consolation to you," he added hesitantly, "take comfort in the fact that the boy Ricky wouldn't have lived out the month anyway, whether he got to your silver or not. And Bill. This was his last night with or without your influence. You don't have to feel guilty about either of them." He turned to leave, and then after a moment's consideration he ended with: "Remember what I asked you last month? About why you actually hated me? Well, I didn't bite you and I didn't kill the Professor. So maybe in time you'll learn not to hate me so much." And with that he was gone, and I was left with a man whom I believed to have been killed, but who was in fact part of the reason for this entire experience.

"We really didn't think it could go on longer than a month," he explained. "We knew you would find some way of keeping yourself awake eventually, and then the jig would be up."

"Why...?" I began, but did not know where to begin, what to actually ask. What did it all come down to, after all?

"I think I got the idea from Bill," he said, and immediately had my attention. "He was a reporter, he was keeping a log of his life and experiences with us. And I guess I thought, 'Wouldn't it be great if he could take his tale to the outside world, tell them about us?' But he couldn't. And just having him send his writings off to some paper or publisher wouldn't do. We needed someone who could actually *return* from their life here with us. With their stories, with their experiences, with their knowledge of who we are and how we live... Someone who could be for us... an ambassador of sorts. Present our desires, explain our needs, speak for us to your kind."

I felt that he thought too much of me, that I was in way over my head. "How do you expect me to—"

"You can't. Not just yet. The first step is to get the word out. If they think it's fiction at first, so be it. There will be those who suspect, and others who will know. And then will be time for step two."

"And how am I supposed to know what to do then?"

"We'll find you and tell you."

"And you trust me?" It was a stupid thing to ask, but I asked it nonetheless.

"What can you do, bring the government down on us? They're already on their way, and we won't be here when they arrive. There'll be no trace of us at all. Unless you want to tell them that we turned into wolves and ran across the land under their very helicopters' noses. But where will that get you? They're not ready for that kind of truth, but it is my hope that in time they will be."

It dawned on me that their existence probably explains all those ghost town mysteries that have been plaguing mankind for years. No, it may not explain how the town's *original* residents were forced to leave, but it should rationalize away those odd peculiarities that have fueled their mystery. Whole towns abandoned at the drop of a hat, with showers still running, food still warm, et cetera. Now it was not so unusual; in fact, it was downright obvious. They were there, they were found out, they took off. Simple. Plain as that.

"Oh, before I forget..." he added, reaching a hand into his back pocket and producing a brown leather book. "Bill's journal. See if you can use it. I don't mean to imply that his insights might be keener than yours; it's just that he *was* here considerably longer, and from what I hear he had a good impression about us, our lifestyle, and even his time among us. If anything, it might be able to help give you an impression of us that isn't tainted by bitterness. You *did* spend most of *your* time here hating both us and the experience, after all. Maybe if we hadn't have tricked you... I don't know. It's like Jack said, no point talking about it now."

There seemed to be a finality to what he said, and in fact he was turning to leave. "Wait!" I blurted out, suddenly not wanting to be alone there.

"Yes?" he said genially, with his casual manner and comfortable smile.

"Well... I mean, that's it? Off ya go? 'Sorry for the month of hell, but you understand, now go do our bidding?' Is that all I get?"

"As I believe you already know, your rent's paid up. You may have to reactivate phone and cable, but that shouldn't be a great hardship. The equivalent of one month's salary has been deposited into your bank account, and as for your job—well, if your employer doesn't agree that you've been working on the story of a lifetime, I'm sure you can find another who will better appreciate what you've been through. Even if they don't believe the particulars of your account, there have been police reports, a missing person's claim... I can't see how anyone could fire you when you've clearly been abducted. And if they don't believe by whom, then they'll just assume you were drugged the whole time and were hallucinating. Your car is not far from your apartment—the police were stumped by that one—and to get home you simply have to ask for a lift from the government agents who find you here. Before they get here, though, you should go free the one down the pit and at least show that you're not one of us, that you were a captive here too. There's a rope ladder tied to a tree not far from the hole. I'm surprised you and Bill didn't find it; it's not hidden all that carefully. There. Now 'that's it.' You're on your own from here on. But don't worry, we'll be back in your life soon enough. Till then, *in bocca al lupo.*"

And then he slowly transformed before taking his leave of me, his clothes falling to the ground in a heap to reveal a beautiful gray wolf, with a silver patch on his head. It was him all along, always there to watch over and protect me. I stood there with my mouth open, and if a wolf could smile he did. He then trotted off to join the rest in their mass exodus to another town, each pack separating and finding its own new home, or perhaps meeting up with another pack to form another community with a new head alpha. And the Hyenas would carry the news along, of Jack and the Professor—Richard—and their experiment with a phony Dingo whom they then returned to the world. Or maybe that would have to wait. They kept saying how they weren't "authorized" to do this. Perhaps the news wouldn't be spilled until the consequences of this action were revealed, *depending* on the outcome. But until then it's all up to me. Do I tell the world about them? How do I go about it?

    The one thing I was sure of was that it was *my* story to tell, no one else's, especially not the federal governments'. And I would tell it on *my* terms. I went into this hoping to become an ace reporter, and I'd be damned if I was about to let anyone take away what I so deservedly earned. After a month of subjugation, *I* now called the shots. I was feeling a high, derived from what felt like the equivalent of suddenly being rescued from certain death—or a fate *worse* than death. No longer having to worry about turning into a monster, losing control three nights a month, fearing being put down if I get too out-of-hand, having my love life restricted and being told that the man I loved was forbidden to me.

    Then the full rush of tonight's events hit me and I realized that the man I loved was still being kept from me—forever!—for he was gunned down in an act that was admittedly merciful and without alternative. And with it came the guilt, though not the same one as before. This time I felt guilty for being alive, and more than that, for rejoicing over my release from the fate we thought we shared. Those plans that only began to take seed in that teacher's lounge would never bear fruit. We would never be together, whether in the *Canis sapien* community or among our own kind, our *original* kind, the human race. And I also felt guilt over not having properly mourned my lover's death, or hardly even thought about it with all the other big news I had to assimilate. Before setting off to do what needed to be done, I returned to the site of Bill's murder and looked at what was left of his body—and the lack of any identifiable feature tore at my heart. I could see how the remains would prove challenging for our medical examiners, but I was not wholly convinced that modern forensics couldn't uncover something from it.

I could hear the sound of helicopters in the distance. I vowed not to let them see me cry, and so I tried to reel in and suppress my emotions, and to collect my thoughts as to what needed to be done next. I first retrieved my diary and other personal effects, carefully avoiding looking into the many cabins with wide-open doors, behind which I knew would be more decaying remains of Dingoes like myself—I mean, Dingoes like I thought myself to be. (I could not believe how hard it was to accept that my nightmare was over and that I was a normal human being after all.) I made my way to the pit where the government man (whose name turned out to be Brian Clemens) was sequestered and easily found the rope ladder in its rather obvious hiding spot by the nearest tree. I called down to him, and when he answered I told him about the ladder and threw it down to him. He climbed up and thanked me, following with a hundred questions about who I was and how I came to be here. "Are you the only one left? Where have they all gone?"

All I could tell him was that they kidnapped me a month ago and kept me drugged, which was true, leaving out a whole lot of the tale. He saw the bruises on my wrists and asked if they had tied me up. I said that they did but that they let me go with instructions to free him before they disappear. And disappear they would, leaving not a trace of human departure, again telling the truth but only a part of it.

He gave me the typical assurances that they would be able to track any man leaving these premises in the past twenty-four hours, much less the past hour, with ease, and his male bravado kicked in as he boasted of their technology and equipment. I watched from the sidelines as the man's associates scoured the whole abandoned community and the surrounding woodlands. There were dogs with them and two Native American "trackers," and I don't know which were more confused. The dogs wouldn't even attempt to follow a trail. Of the two trackers, the younger one simply wore an expression of bafflement, while the older one (by many moons) kept a somber tone and occasionally glanced my way as if hoping I would confirm some unspoken suspicion. I had no doubt that Native Americans knew of the *Canis sapiens*, at least in legends and fables, but surely only the older generations would give any credence to them, the younger ones being just as jaded as I and the rest of my history-less, nationality-neutral, generic-brand generation.

I met the old Indian's eyes but kept my gaze noncommittal. I fought back a tear that threatened to emerge, but I wasn't sure if it was caused by my mental state or by the strain of maintaining my neutral composure. The search looked like it would continue well after I was driven home — not by Brian Clemens, whose general health and condition was being looked after, but by his superior, a lean, middle-aged, silver-haired man named "Smith," who grilled me back at my place much more efficiently than his subordinate, but with no greater success.

When I was finally alone in my apartment, the first light of dawn began shining through the Eastward-facing windows. I dropped both journals onto my bedside table and collapsed onto my bed for a well-deserved slumber. I dreamt of my recent experiences, but none of my dreams could ever be more bizarre or terrifying than what I actually lived through. Faces flooded my vision, faces belonging to people who up until a few hours ago were living, breathing, healthy individuals, some of whom I had grown to care deeply about. Bill Jensen, Ricky Hasselhoff, and Wendy Summers were just a few of the faces that visited me; there was also Samantha... Maverick, I believe her last name was, and the rest of the girls in Jezebel's brothel whom until recently I had simply thought of as Dingo prostitutes but whom I now knew by name. There was Jessica Walters, a prestigious lawyer in her human life who embraced both Dingo life and her new profession with surprising ease and fervor; Ellen Danbury and Jackie Royster, whose previous professions escaped me at the moment; Roslyn... DeMayo, who was a prostitute for human customers before taking on her new — preferred — clientele; and... I was ashamed and disappointed to find that I couldn't remember the names of the rest of the girls; I would have to reacquaint myself with them through Bill's writing.

But Dingoes weren't the only ones I dreamt about. There was dear, understanding Jezebel; alpha Jack, whom I no longer knew how I felt about; Richard, who would forever be "the Professor" to me; and even Aryana, another one whose treatment toward me was so inconsistent that I knew not how to feel about her.

. . . . .

Waking sometime before noon, I grabbed up my diary to pen the final pages to this initial tale. Intent on returning to sleep — for at least most of the day — I would later address all those things that need to be addressed. There were calls to make, people to assure, decisions to weigh, losses to mourn. But right now, there was sleep to make up.

Purchase other Black Rose Writing titles at www.blackrosewriting.com/books
and use promo code PRINT to receive a 20% discount.

BLACK ROSE
writing™

Made in the USA
San Bernardino, CA
14 April 2016